Remembering Zion

Remembering Zion

A Spiritual Love Novel

Morley David Glicken

iUniverse, Inc.
New York Lincoln Shanghai

Remembering Zion

A Spiritual Love Novel

iUniverse books may be ordered through booksellers or by contacting:

iUniverse
2021 Pine Lake Road, Suite 100
Lincoln, NE 68512
www.iuniverse.com
1-800-Authors (1-800-288-4677)

ISBN-13: 978-0-595-36373-5 (pbk)
ISBN-13: 978-0-595-80810-6 (ebk)
ISBN-10: 0-595-36373-3 (pbk)
ISBN-10: 0-595-80810-7 (ebk)

Printed in the United States of America

Author's Greeting

I wrote *Remembering Zion* because I wanted to show the spiritual side of love and the way it can shape our view of the world around us. For those of you who believe in *Beshert*, the notion that for everybody there is a chosen one with whom we can achieve an immortal love, I hope you find this novel as touching to read as it was for me to write.

The book is composed of two separate, but interconnected novellas, *Remembering Zion* and *The City of Eternal Spring*. Both novellas are about spiritual love and the characters in the first novella continue on in the second. The book comes shortly after the publication of a book I wrote about men and women: *Ending the Sex Wars: A Woman's Guide to Understanding Men,* also published by iuniverse. In that book I discuss the ways in which men and women can resolve difficult interpersonal problems, while in this novel I've tried to show how people, in the midst of very difficult personal times, can work through their difficulties and still find a deeply personal love.

I realize that it can be misleading to use the word "spiritual" in describing a novel, but as I wrote *Remembering Zion* in the mountains of Utah, with Deer and Moose visiting my cabin, it felt as if the book was being dictated to me. You may say that the book was inside of me all of the time and that when it was ready to write itself, it did. But I think the spiritual side of us, the side that searches for meaning exists because God is in all of us, gently nudging us to do the creative and important things in life that give us meaning. I still feel His presence when I read the book and I hope that *Remembering Zion* will lead you in safe, loving, and tender directions.

God Bless!
Morley David Glicken

Book One

Remembering Zion

Prologue

Sometime in the night, a vision came to me. It was a vision of Zion National Park in southern Utah and the towers of granite and sandstone that rise from prehistoric oceans and form the enchanted sacred walls of that beautiful place. I have been there many times, but in my vision, it looked different in the way that dreams make the common place slightly surreal.

I saw many splendid things in my vision, but the most wonderful thing I saw was the birth of a child. I did not know whose child it was, but I can remember that I was astonished when she was born. It felt like the rebirth of the world when I saw her tiny body.

And then she grew up before my eyes and it was my Jennifer, suddenly a grown and beautiful woman. She beckoned to me and I touched her hand. It was warm and soft to the touch. She held me and we listened to someone preach from the sandstone formation known as the Pulpit, which is in the Valley of the Patriarchs.

I do not remember the person who spoke, but his words ring true to me, even now. What he said was:

"Do not grieve for loved ones who are no longer with us. Each day brings with it the possibilities of new love. Permit your heart to be receptive and do not discount the opportunities, because love is like a mighty river. It cannot be stopped, but flows through us and goes its own course."

His majestic voice surrounded everything and hung from the tops of the canyons and filled the Valley of the Patriarchs like thunder.

"Be appreciative of every opportunity God presents us," he said. "Never turn those away with whom you may truly find happiness. Be gentle as the spring wind with those who are dear to you, and sing the praises of God each day. For God is great and he will protect and care for us all, every one of us, for we are his children."

It is strange that I can remember what he said in the dream as clearly as if he'd said it this minute. Perhaps I remember the dream so vividly because it is what I believe. Perhaps the speaker in my dream touched my heart and fashioned his sermon from my thoughts and feelings. I don't know, but when I am very sad, when things go badly and I feel so lonely that it is like a knife inside my heart to go on with another day, I hear the words of that secret preacher and they soothe me.

I worship at the alter of love. I praise God for giving us such a sublime experience. I hope, with all that is within me, that it will happen again and again until I am too old to love, and then I hope it happens to me then, as well.

We are so afraid of love, I think. We have a bad love and we would do anything not to repeat the pain. And yet, love is wonderful beyond measure when it is right and true. It is a majesty of wonder and a bounty of feelings that we all crave.

In many ways, I feel like a wanderer in time and space. I am here with everyone, but my heart and soul are elsewhere. They are with the special women who captured my heart and made life more bearable for an aging man.

For them, and for all the women of the world who reach out and touch the hearts of men, I write this experience of the heart and spirit.

CHAPTER 1

I don't know why I drove hundreds of miles out of my way to spend the night in Zion National Park. I'd been there so many times before that, long ago, I had seen everything there was to see. And being by myself, the canyons, in all of their glory, left me feeling more lonely than ever. I should have driven as directly as I could to my summer job in North Dakota, avoiding this place and all of its memories.

And yet, I was drawn here, drawn to see the place where we met, held hands, kissed on the wooden swing by the pool, and fell in love the first few minutes we were together. It was, and is, a love so deeply personal that I have trouble thinking that I could ever completely understand what took place in that remarkable year we were together. But there I was, back where we met for the first time, reliving the times we spent in Zion.

I sat in our very special room in the early heat of summer, tired from the drive, and yet flooded with bitter sweet memories of the many times Jennifer and I came to Zion. It was our meeting place, our special place, halfway between her home in Utah and mine in California.

Our room hadn't changed in the four years since we were here last or, for that matter, since I first met Jennifer in late summer before our children returned to school. Accidentally, of course, for some things happen that way. Jennifer always believed that had we met anyplace else, we would not have fallen in love or spent the wonderful, and then ultimately sad year we had together.

One year. A lifetime. An eternity. A poet once said that, "In love's timetable, a moment is forever."

I believe that now because without Jennifer in my life, days have begun to take on the sadness of a lifetime and nights are filled with dreams I wish I could forget.

I was 45 that summer when we met. If the great weariness of mid-life was obvious to me, I don't remember. But I know that I was all but burned out; on work, on love, maybe even on life.

I had my daughter Rachel for the summer, of course, my 10 year-old, a child to make any father proud of whatever magic God creates when children are born. I had a good job teaching, a few dollars saved, a new home, my health. I should have been happy, but I wasn't. In that moment of my life, I'd lost my faith that I would ever love again.

Say what you will, but to stop believing that you will ever feel the sweet joy of love, or long for someone, or ache in the night to touch someone you love is one of the worst sorrows you can have in life. When people say that someone died of a broken heart, it's the same thing. They died because they stopped believing that they would fall in love again.

To love a child isn't the same. A child loves you back, unconditionally. They don't ask you to be their dad or mom, you just are. If you've been wise and gentle in your love for them, they love you back. An adult needs another adult to love, someone whose opinion is so completely determined by their love for us that anything we do is splendid and wonderful beyond comprehension.

Forty-five years-old and I had no one in my life who felt that way about me. Maybe I'd begun to believe that no one would ever feel that way about me again and that love was dead.

Loneliness, if you've never been there, is everything it's cracked up to be. To not have someone touch you, warm and tender, to go to bed yet again by yourself, to eat another lonely meal while watching T.V. with no one to ask how your day went, to sit staring at the walls of your room wishing that someone would fall magically into your life knowing, of course, that it would never happen, all of it is like a slow, bloodless death.

Your child comes for the summer and, for a moment, a nano-second, really, you forget about your loneliness. No, you don't really forget it. You tuck it away in a corner of your heart so that you can be as good as you can possibly be with your child. You put away the fatigue, the heartbreak, and the fear of death without someone to be with you in the end, and you paint a happy face over the one that usually looks morose. You go on the trips you talk about taking during the year even if you're tired and burned out from yet another loveless, backbreaking year of work and never ending loneliness, which is what I did with Rachel the summer I met Jennifer.

Rachel and I left early one morning in mid-August, in the smog of a California summer, for the North Rim of the Grand Canyon, a place of such beauty that it made you want to exalt in the world, to sing the praises of God.

Jennifer, as it would turn out, was also there when we were. But, for whatever reasons God has for these things, we didn't see her in the three days we spent in our little log cabin with gophers running across Rachel in the morning to wake her from her 10 year-old sleep.

I think about that now as some sort of divine message. The North Rim is small. It would be difficult to miss someone as beautiful as Jennifer, or as tall. She was almost my height and she could look into my eyes, head on. It's a very special thing to see someone's eyes so clearly and to not have to bend down when you kiss them. When she spoke to me the first time, I couldn't get words to come out of my mouth.

That Jennifer and her son were there exactly at the same time as Rachel and I makes me wonder about the way God works his magic. We saw the very same things, went to the same lectures, and ate in the same restaurant. On different days and at different times. Maybe Jennifer was right. We wouldn't have had the same impact on each other had it not been for us meeting later at the pool in Zion.

I finally did get the words to come out that first time we met. What's so strange is that after I got to know her a little, I could talk to her about anything. She would fix me with that out of focus look of hers and the words would come out of my mouth as if I was possessed. Maybe I was.

I could talk to her about my father, who had just died, and with whom I'd had a troubled and difficult relationship. I spoke to her about my work and the growing lethargy I felt for it. I told her about my writing and the poetry that seemed to be coming out of my head as if somebody were dictating it to my hands.

Shyly, at first, because I distrusted my ability to write, and then I wrote her a poem, uncomfortable, critical of my ability, and gave it to her and watched her cry as she read it. It was the single most wonderful moment of my life until then because I wrote it at the pool in Zion and it seemed to flow out of me as if it were locked in time waiting for me to grab hold of it and catch it. I wrote it on the back of a library due date card. It said:

> If I should ever love you as much as I am able
> Then, we will be in love for an eternity
> And I will surely live inside of your heart
> And enter your soul.

CHAPTER 2

Prophetic words since I had known her less than twenty minutes at the time and didn't know then, as I was to learn later, that she was married.

She cried when she read the poem, and then she blushed and said that she had to leave for awhile because she was too emotional to sit with me and not make a fool of herself.

Later, she would come back and kiss me on the lips, a long kiss, a kiss I won't forget as long as I live. I could feel hot tears in my mouth and then I felt her quiver. Or was it me?

I can't tell you why any of this happened. Perhaps we were both waiting for that one true and perfect love or, maybe, in those days when we were at the North Rim of the Grand Canyon and kept missing one another, our spirits met and fell in love before our bodies caught up.

I don't know. All I can say is that in the moment when she kissed me full on the mouth, I changed. And so did the world around me. It seemed, somehow....nicer, kinder. Rachel adored her from the moment she met Jennifer and told me later, "That's the one, dad."

But I didn't need Rachel to tell me. I knew it as we stood in the pool talking as if we'd known each other forever.

She asked me if I thought an abusive parent affected people into adulthood. Was she talking about her son, I wondered? No, she was talking about herself. She was talking about a father who made her so uncomfortable when he was near her that she had to leave the room, often in a panic. And she was having dreams, frightening dreams of someone touching her, violating her.

I told her that this was not a conversation for strangers in a pool. She needed to talk to a professional. And then she looked me full in the eyes, in that disarming out of focus way of hers, with those beautiful eyes and said, just a few minutes into our relationship, "When you love someone, Sam, nothing should be so disturbing that you can't talk about it."

I looked at her for the longest time, this beautiful woman, this glorious person I'd just met and I said to her," Are you saying you love me?"

She just looked away and then she touched my face and said, "I don't need to tell you something you already know."

And then, God help me, I babbled. Partly because it's what I do for a living...I'm a professor of psychology...and partly because I was so dazzled by her that I didn't want her to leave. I wanted her to stay by me forever, her breasts softly touching my chest. I wanted to look at her eyes, and listen to her voice, and watch the way her mouth formed words. I was so taken with her that the world could have come to an end and I wouldn't have noticed.

When I finished ranting the psychobabble I teach in my classes about abusive parents and the harm they do to their children, she said, simply, "Thank you. I know what I need to do now."

It may seem to you that a discussion of abuse minutes into knowing someone was an indication of trouble to come, but that's the way Jennifer was, to the point and very direct. What troubled her at the moment was what she needed to discuss. She never spoke to me about her father again, at least not directly.

When Rachel and I were in the North Rim, we went to an isolated place for a picnic. It rained for awhile, black clouds covering the canyon, and we stayed in the car waiting for the rain to let up. When the rain was over, a beautiful rainbow stretched across the canyon from rim to rim.

We got out of the car and sat at a wet picnic table on the canyon rim eating our meal when three curious deer walked up to our table and sniffed us. Rachel still talks about it to this day. It seemed to me that the entire trip was filled with magic.

Another time we went to an old Anasazi ruin on the canyon rim and listened to a ranger discuss that ancient and mysterious tribe of early Native Americans. They'd built magnificent dwellings all over the southwest. And then one day, for reasons no one can explain, they mysteriously vanished leaving their enormous and beautifully conceived dwellings in Chaco Canyon and Mesa Verde and hundreds of thousands of other places, absolutely empty. We can only gawk at them now and wonder why such a thing could ever happen. But perhaps, as with all beautiful things, conflicts and misunderstandings and the way we humans have of driving one another away caught up with them and they could no longer live together.

Which is exactly what Rachel said to me as the ranger began to talk about the disappearance of the Anasazi. "Maybe they just couldn't get along anymore," she whispered, "and they decided to break up and live somewhere else." A fellow tourist turned to us and said that it was the best explanation he had ever heard. He turned out to be a world famous anthropologist showing his grandchildren Anasazi ruins that summer.

That's the way our trip to the canyon went, full of the fun of adventure that goes along with a child's discovery of the world. Jennifer said the same thing about her experiences with her son. Maybe God sprinkled some magic potent over the Grand Canyon that week and watched on high as people fell in love.

After the Grand Canyon, we drove through the rain to the general store at Jacob Lake before driving on to Zion. Everyone told us that the muffins at Jacob Lake were exceptional, and so they were. Jennifer, driving at the same time, also stopped at Jacob Lake for muffins. We did not meet.

Rachel squealed as we ran to the general store in the rain. It seemed all too wonderful. Having grown up with the dark influences of a European father who believed that anything really good could only be followed by something really terrible, I distrusted life when it went too well. We ate in the car, the muffins slightly soggy from the rain, but delicious beyond description. It is these moments I remember in my life with Rachel. They are the moments of rebirth and reaffirmation that make being a parent so wonderful.

I can remember sitting in the car in the rain watching squirrels run through the pine trees and seeing, out of the corner of an eye, a moose walk slowly out of the woods. The single act of seeing something so wild and free filled me with a joy I cannot describe. Maybe being released from city life and the squalor of California was the best tonic anyone could have. And, of course, to share it with your child was something you never forget.

The moose stared at us for a moment, threw his large head back, and walked nonchalantly back into the woods. I looked over at Rachel. She had an astonished look on her face. It was a look, I think, of utter happiness and contentment.

Chapter 3

Five years later in my room in Zion, I looked at the pool where we met. Unlike the day we'd met five years ago, the pool was deserted. I walked around the complex waiting for Jennifer to come out of our room and hold me and tell me that everything was fine, but, of course, everything wasn't fine. I was alone now and I didn't believe, deep down inside of myself, that I would ever stop being alone. It made me more lonely and sad than I can describe.

I sat at a picnic bench when a dog ran up to me and licked my hand. I touched his face and ran my hand under his chin. He rolled over and wanted me to touch his stomach. For some reason, the simple trick made me cry and I walked back to the room, afraid that someone would see me.

Sitting in my room, my mind jumped back five years and I remembered that first day at the pool when Jennifer told me that she was married. She didn't tell me the awful details to help me understand the terrible things I would find out later about her marriage. All she said was, "I'm married, Sam. You should know that."

When you're in love and you haven't loved in so long that you can't remember what it's even like anymore, you hang on to your new love because you believe that you won't get another chance.

When Jennifer said she was married, I didn't vacillate or run with Rachel back to California like any sane person would have done. No, I told myself that it didn't matter and that I could deal with it. But it did matter, of course.

Not right away. Right away it would have taken elephants to separate us. We were so hungry for each other that nothing could have come between us.

Later that evening, after the children were asleep, we met by the wooden swing near the pool and made brave plans to see each other in the future. And we kept those plans even though we knew it was wrong of us.

Funny how you can put important issues away when you have love on your side. I didn't think that what we were planning was wrong or that someone might get hurt. I was so desperate for love that I would have kissed her in front of the Pope or declared my love for her publicly on talk radio.

Did you feel it right away when you met the person you would love? I did. The moment I saw her, I knew I was in love. She did, too.

Before I met Jennifer, I would have told my psychology students that love at first sight was really just lust at first sight, but I was wrong. The first moment I saw Jennifer, I knew I loved her. A wave of emotion came over me and I felt weak and dizzy and happy, all at the same time. But it had nothing at all to do with lust. I loved her and I could not even remember feeling the deep and profound longing I would have for her after we made love for the first time.

What I felt when we made love the first time was a feeling so deep inside of me, so passionately, indescribably gentle and tender, that it felt as if I was being carried away in space and time. Like the old song, it felt as if I was on the wings of some wondrous bird, flying toward heaven.

> On the wings of a snow white dove,
> He sends his pure, sweet love.
> A sign from above,
> on the wings of a dove.

We cried in each other's arms when we made love the first time. The feelings were so strong and true, it was like a dam breaking.

Who guides us in matters of love? I wish that I'd had a mentor, a wise person to help me over the hurdles. But there was no one, as there is always no one when we need wisdom and guidance. My friends would not have understood. How do you explain that you love someone you hardly know to people who think that such conduct is for teenagers or that it's surely a sign of your weak character? I couldn't bring myself to talk to anyone about Jennifer. Love was new territory for me. The road seemed straight and certain and I didn't think that I would lose my way.

"I'm married," Jennifer said again as we sat on the wooden swing at night, after the children were asleep. Then she leaned over and kissed me with a long, sweet kiss that made me feel like swinging through the trees and thumping my chest.

I don't remember saying anything of consequence after she told me she was married because she quickly added, "And it won't matter, Sam, because when you love someone like I love you, it can't possibly matter."

She held my hand as the night bugs flew every which way but didn't touch us as if they were on special orders from God. She held my hand and then she told me enough about her marriage for me to understand why it didn't matter.

But it did matter to me. It sat in my heart and I felt, of all things, jealous. In truth, I didn't want to share her with anybody, not even her husband.

"Don't feel badly, Sam. We'll do fine. You'll see," she said, and I believed her with all my heart.

Those thoughts came back to me in a rush as I sat by the pool in Zion five years later, alone, tired, and so very, very sad. I went for a swim before it got too cold outside, but the memories left me feeling morose. After awhile, I got out of the pool and decided that the water wouldn't cure my sadness or mend my broken heart. There is no baptismal for lonely lovers.

At dusk, I watched the jet planes so high over-head that they were soundless. The trails of vapor in the clear late afternoon sky were like streaks across the sun, or a moonbeam at night. I told Jennifer to look up but, of course, I was just talking to myself and to the dog who sat outside the fence and looked at me, forlorn and lonely. Just, dear God, like me.

I remembered a poem I wrote for Jennifer in the early morning on one of our visits to Zion.

> Who could ever know how much I love you,
> or care for you in tender moments
> when our hearts are one
> and we cry out in the night.
> Tender moments to treasure.

Chapter 4

Back to the trip Rachel and I took that summer I first met Jennifer. From Jacob Lake, Rachel and I drove down the mountain from the Grand Canyon through the dismal town of Fredonia and to the beautiful Mormon community of Kanab. It was a town where many cowboy movies had been made in the 1950's and in the lobby of the main hotel, you could see pictures of a young John Wayne laughing and joking with the hotel owners. There was something very sad about the pictures since many of the people we saw, all of them famous stars, had died of cancer twenty years later. Because Kanab was in a direct line of the wind that carried the radioactive particles from the Nevada test sites where atom bombs were exploded regularly, many people thought that the sand near Kanab was radioactive. It made me feel particularly nervous that we'd walked and picked stones from the ground in this same area.

Past Kanab, we turned off Highway 89A and drove the 15 miles to see the Pink Coral Sand Dunes, magnificent dunes in the middle of the Utah wilderness with so few visitors that the park rangers had long ago left and the walk through the dunes was done on the honor system. We walked across dunes as high as 200 feet, bright pink and shifting in the morning wind. I wished we had a camel to ride on and imagined the two of us dressed like Lawrence of Arabia, trekking through the sand on a secret mission to some sacred, and splendid, and mysterious city in the Sahara desert. But then a plane flew high overhead and we could see cars on the road as they drove by.

Thunderclouds spread across the sky as we walked to our car and suddenly it rained as hard as I've ever seen it rain in the desert. We drove to high ground and watched sheets of water hit the windshield of our car and the dry streams that lay dormant suddenly filled with torrents of water. I'd never seen anything like it before. Where once it was dry and lifeless, water suddenly rushed down empty riverbeds, filling the narrow channels and washing everything away in its place. We later heard that the famous old hotel in Kanab with the pictures of John Wayne had been flooded and that five inches of rain fell in an hour. Watching the carnage made me want to hug Rachel until she couldn't move. Life is precious, and in a moment it can change and leave you empty.

When the rain stopped and the water subsided, we drove carefully down the rutted highway still full of water and saw several cars that had been washed away. We saw no one and could only hope that the cars were the empty and vacant leftovers of the past, the junked out remains of life so common in the desert. By the time we reached the highway to Cortez Junction, the sun was out and we could see the white cliffs in the distance that reminded me of the cowboy movies I was so addicted to as a kid. In Cortez Junction, we stopped at a local fruit stand and bought cherries, and apple cider, and Utah plumbs as big and as juicy as small apples. Rachel, eating one, sprayed me with juice and we laughed until we couldn't stop. I remember a woman watching us and thinking I should say hello, but I didn't. Was it Jennifer? I'd like to think so but maybe it was just another tourist like us, alone in the summer, doing the trips single parents do with their kids, wondering if the loneliness would come back when the summer was over.

We turned on to highway 9 to Zion National Park, the only regular highway in the country to charge a fee since it went right through the park. You paid whether you stayed or if you were on your way to someplace else.

The road gradually rose and soon we were in ponderosa and high desert shrub. After the ranger booth where we paid our fee we could see the ripples in the white sandstone, ripples made by a prehistoric sea which once covered the entire area. Not far from here in Vernal and Moab, Utah were the huge petrified dinosaur bones found in the rocks and which were excavated for the public to see, and no movie could ever do justice to the size and majesty of those creatures.

The road continued to rise and soon we went through the first of several very long tunnels with rows of cars, trucks, and motor homes crawling their way through dimly lit caverns. Every few hundred feet we could see out the windows carved out of the mountains by the men and women who worked the WPA projects that had built the park in the 1930's. You wondered about these folks and how they could do such incredible things and the dignity it must have given them to create such beauty in the midst of the poverty and unemployment of the depression years.

And then we were in Zion, in the main lodge, and the majesty and grandeur was more than I could believe. Rachel sat starring at the cliffs, afraid to speak, I think, for fear they would go away and that it was a dream.

CHAPTER 5

Her maiden name was Jennifer Young. She preferred to go by that name rather than her married one. She taught languages at a high school in Salt Lake City. Somewhere down the pike, her great, great grandfather was Brigham Young, a very big deal if you're a Mormon. And Jennifer was a Mormon, but very, very lapsed, as she would have said. She called herself a "Jack Mormon," a reference to someone of the faith who was not active.

Her son Ryan was six when we met, a blond boy of such natural beauty that it took your breath away to look at him. Jennifer's husband was a businessman and an alcoholic, a serious problem in any case, but particularly serious for a Mormon because of the restrictions they place on drinking. She was 34 the first time we met in Zion and a Leo. Odd. So was Rachel's mom.

She married right out of high school and thought that she loved her husband until the drinking got in the way. By then, the marriage had begun the slow descent into boredom and lethargy that marks all too many American marriages in this the era of the broken home and the broken heart.

This is the way that Jennifer told it to me, simple and straight forward. Just the facts, Sam. Later, I learned that the facts were slightly skewed to protect the innocent, and that Jennifer had an early life to make us psychologists rich. Not to mention the fact that her husband, Jason, could be abusive when the spirits struck. And that, as I found out later, could be often.

She was tall. For the record, 5-10. She was the former Rodeo Queen in some county in Utah where that was important, and then the queen of a lot of other things. She was beautiful and full bodied. *Zophtig*, as my Jewish mother would have said. She had nice legs, a great set of eyes, long brown hair as fine as silk, and a sensuality about her that was positively overpowering.

It was, at least on the surface, an innocent sensuality. Like many abused children, Jennifer was so out of touch with what had been done to her and the damage it would cause that she hadn't a clue about how she affected men. Her husband thought that she was unfaithful, but until me, she had been scrupulously faithful.

She was a wonderful companion. We explored the most beautiful places in Utah together. We saw the awesome spires at Bryce Canyon and the impossible rock formations at Arches National Park. Once we saw the beautiful and eerie country near Moab where the Colorado River winds its way through the rocks creating gigantic and wonderful formations that make you think of some lunar landscape. We also went down the river on a raft and threw water at each other until we were as brown as the river water. As we passed the rocks along the Colorado, we could see petrogliffs etched in the rock by ancient Native Americans. Our guide pointed at depressions in the rock and told us that they were dinosaur foot-prints which had petrified over time.

We were in love and every moment in our relationship is etched into my memory, just like the Indian paintings or the dinosaur foot prints we saw on our trip down the Colorado.

I saw Jennifer again, less than a month after we first met at Zion. We made love together, one night, and if I never make love again, it will not displease me. Until then, I really hadn't loved anyone enough to say that I'd made love to them.

It was during the first two weeks of September and just before the start of the fall quarter. I rented a log cabin for two weeks in the resort area in the mountains outside of Salt Lake called Park City. When I was married, we spent summers in Park City to get away from the mid-west heat. Now, tired and soul weary, I'd come back to that peaceful place to try and renew myself before I went back to my students and the academic demands of the coming year.

Jennifer called me one morning early in my stay. She'd gotten my number from the rental company I told her I would be using. "Hi, Sam," she said, "remember me?"

"Hi, Jennifer," I said back, not knowing exactly what to say after you've told someone you loved them and then hadn't seen them in a month or called them as you'd promised you would.

"Do you still love me, Sam?" she asked.

"I do," I said, feeling very self-conscious and guilty. The truth was, I hadn't called her because I thought she'd forgotten me and that she'd laugh away our moments together as just a great infatuation. Say what you will about men, but when it comes to confidence about women, most of us haven't gone beyond the 6th grade in our understanding of love, romance, and women..

"Do you really, Sam?" she asked. "Don't say that to me unless you really mean it, Sam."

I closed my eyes so that I could see her as she looked the first time I ever saw her. She was wearing a swimming suit and my heart was pounding like crazy. Please come and be with me, my heart was saying, I think I'm in love with you. And then I told her what she said to me when we first met: "I don't need to tell you, Jennifer, something you already know."

She came later in the day. We sat on the balcony and watched the sun go down and the colors flaming across the western sky like a fireball. As the sun went down and twilight turned the sky to a dark purple, she made me promise that I would be faithful to her or we couldn't make love. She made me write it down like a contract and then promise, crisscross my heart. She said that if I broke my promise, we wouldn't ever see each other again and that fidelity, when you're in love, is like a vow to God.

It seemed a strange thing for someone who was married to say, but maybe she was right. Maybe the way we felt for each other made everything else in our lives irrelevant.

I felt like I was 15 when we made love, like it was new and wise and profound. I felt that way, I think, because it was like making love for the very first time.

The river is wide, I cannot see.
Nor do I have wide wings to fly.
Build me a boat that will carry two,
and both shall roam, my love and I.

CHAPTER 6

Five years later, as I revisited the place where we had first met, the memories wouldn't stop coming. I laid on the bed where we'd slept together so many times before and felt my heart begin to hurt from all the memories. I remembered the last time we were together in Zion, when Jennifer cried and the pillow was wet with sweet tears and her hair smelled like roses and violets and other flowers I couldn't identify.

My mind was racing as I laid there on our bed. It felt as if Jennifer was next to me and that her breasts touched my chest and her nipples were hard against my skin. Not having her in my life seemed like a cruel joke God was playing on me.

What a trickster God can be. He gives us the greatest thing he ever created and then he takes it away from us and makes it impossible to ever have it again. I didn't care for God in that moment of grief in my life. I didn't care for him at all.

Later that evening, I walked to a local bar and restaurant called the "Bit N' Spur." The dog at the motel followed me to the porch where the cowboys stood drinking "Rollin' Rock Beer" and the women all wore jeans so tight you thought the seams would split. The dog sat by the porch and watched me through the corner of his eye.

Jennifer and I often came here to slow dance. I couldn't take my eyes off the dance floor inside. A tall woman built like Jennifer was slow dancing with a cowboy to a sad Ian Tyson song. The words of the song went:

> There's a young boy that I know,
> just turned twenty-one.
> Comes from down in southern Colorado.

Just out of the service, and he's lookin for some fun.
Some day soon, going with him, some day soon.

My parents cannot stand him cause he works the rodeo.
They say he'll walk away and leave me cryin.
But I would follow him right down
the roughest road of all,
some day soon, going with him, some day soon.

I watched the cowboy dancing with the tall woman in tight jeans and my heart felt like it would break. I wanted Jennifer to walk up to me and take me in her arms and dance with me, slow and easy, as if our bodies were melded together and our love shined through like some eternal beacon in the night to let others know that love was a wonderful gift and we shouldn't squander it.

Instead, I stood there feeling lonely and sorry for myself, so lonely and sorry that I couldn't stay any longer. The dog wagged his tail when he saw me coming, happy that I'd walk with him, oblivious to my sorrow.

When we were together, Jennifer would laugh at my efforts to dance. In a good-natured sort of way because it would have been difficult to imagine Jennifer being mean spirited about anything.

"Sam, honey," she'd say, trying to avoid my shoe on her foot, "I swear, you are the worst dancer I've ever known. Luckily, sugar, you have other redeeming qualities a nice girl could never discuss in so public a place."

The dog and I started walking home and I remembered her saying that to me. I looked up and I could see the sun setting low over the canyons. The air felt as cold as my heart. In the sky above, I could see the vapors of another plane and wondered if anyone else was as lonely as I was. As we walked back to the motel, other memories came back to me in a rush.

When Rachel and I were at the North Rim of the Grand Canyon, we looked for fossils in the rocks. Rachel was just at the point in her life where discovery was very exciting. I remembered seeing a very tall woman out of the corner of my eye. Maybe it was Jennifer.

We walked back to the motel, the dog and I, my head down. Why was I doing this? Why had I come here? It all seemed so painful and unnecessary to relive the past when the past had been so awful.

I was doing it, I reminded myself, because my life had stopped when our relationship had ended. Stopped dead. Maybe returning to Zion after all of these years would give me the answer I so desperately needed. Why had Jennifer stopped loving me?

When she wouldn't see me anymore, it was everything I could do to force myself out of bed for months on end. In time it got better, but a sadness settled over me where it had been hiding out for the past four years. A colleague I respected said that retracing our relationship by going to Zion might help. Here I was, retracing like crazy. It wasn't much fun and it wasn't really helping.

The dog and I sat on the swing by the pool for awhile, watching the colors across the canyon cliffs change into shades of reds and purple. At least I was watching. The dog was watching me. He looked concerned. I could understand that. Jennifer once said that when I was sad, I looked like some stray dog down on his luck.

After she told me she was married and how things were in her marriage, she took my hand and looked at me. "Sam, you're a straight shooter, aren't you? It bothers you that I'm married."

I nodded. It was all I could do. The lump in my throat was that big.

"Maybe once in lifetime, baby, you meet someone. It's the someone you should have met when you were young, the great love, Sam. I've just met him, baby, my great love, and I won't let you leave me. Not now."

I looked at her, at this beautiful woman full of health, full of life, and all I could do was nod.

We sat looking at the fireflies and the moon, and then she said to me, "You can't let me down, Sam. It would break my heart if you did."

"I won't, Jen," I said, and we sat on the very swing I sat on now, holding one another until dawn, talking about our lives as if we'd known one another forever. It was the single most intimate moment I had ever had up to that point in my life.

I shook my head and the memory of Jennifer floated off into space. The dog looked at me funny. I felt my face and realized that there were tears in my eyes. Just another emotional old man, I thought to myself. You and me, dog, just two old has-beens. The dog yawned.

Another memory flickered through my mind, sinister and dark. I tried to stop it from happening, but it came anyway.

We were on our second visit to Zion in early October, sitting at the top of Angles Landing, looking at the incredible view.

"I did what I had to do with my dad, Sam," she said. "I killed him in my mind. He's dead now and he won't bother me anymore."

I turned to look at her, but her face was as blank as a Chinese Death mask. I asked her what she meant, but she only shook her head and put her finger over my lips. "You can't always heal people, my doctor," she said. "Sometimes they won't heal. Sometimes they want to strike back and hurt the people who hurt them, even if it's childish and they know better."

We sat looking at the great vista below and the Virgin River snaking its way across the canyon floor like molten gold and the people below so small that they looked like ants.

"Promise you won't leave me, Sam," she said. "Promise me good and I'll make love to you tonight, and if it doesn't break your heart to think that we'll be away from each other for a month, then it'll break mine."

And she kissed me on the cheek and hummed a song I'd never heard before. Something mournful and sad.

I met her father once, a benign old man with the light extinguished from him so long ago that I wondered if it had been there to begin with. I could not see this man abusing a fly. What do you say to someone you love so much? Later, I met her mother and knew, of course, that if there had been abuse, where it had come from.

The memories floated in and out at will. I couldn't stop them and they had a mind of their own and came and went as they pleased.

It was getting dark now. I watched the fireflies sending mating messages in some code too complex for anyone to understand. After a time, I went to my room feeling sad and angry that I was here alone and that it hurt so much to remember the many things in my life with Jennifer that I thought had been put to rest.

Be with me tonight, Jen, I said to the empty room. Be with me and make love to me, slow and sweet, like only you can do. Don't let me go to bed alone.

And an angel came down from heaven and made it happen in my dreams, and I slept peacefully for the first time since I'd last seen Jennifer. During the night, I heard the dog bark once outside of my room, but the rest of the night I was in a trance, and Jennifer held me and comforted me as I slept the peaceful sleep of someone in love.

Another poem I wrote for Jennifer, but much later.

> I have known your love, and
> if there is anything more dear,
> more special,
> it cannot be of this place.

Perhaps, my love,
we are in heaven with the angels
and we will lie together in peace,
and feel God's special gifts.

CHAPTER 7

The next morning, while it was still cool, I drove the few miles from the motel in Springdale to Zion National Park. I wanted to walk the Narrows Trail where the Virgin River cuts deep into the cliffs and creates a river narrows with cliffs thousands of feet high and no sandy beach to run to if a wall of water comes crashing down the river after a summer rain. The dog wasn't there to greet me. In my loneliness, I missed him almost as much as I missed Jennifer.

The park was not crowded this early in the morning. Most of the tourists come in the afternoon when it was too hot to hike. Jennifer and I walked the Narrows Trail the first time we met alone in Zion in early October. When the trail ended, we put on our worn sneakers and walked up the gorge as far as we could go until the cold mountain water made our bodies numb and the fear of a flash flood from rains in the high mountains forced us back.

The trail was empty, but the walk tired me. After awhile, I stopped and sat on a rock, remembering all too clearly our meeting that Friday afternoon in October, our first time together alone in Zion.

I saw her from a distance and we ran to one another and embraced, kissing each other over and over, laughing like children, walking as fast as we could to the room to make love.

It was a weekend made in heaven. Anything that good doesn't leave your mind, try as hard as you might to forget.

I sat for awhile on the Narrows Trail and nodded at the people as they passed. A cloud passed over the sun and for a moment, there was a chill in the air that went right through me and made me shiver. Another black memory passed by and I covered my eyes so it would end, but it wouldn't and it kept on coming by.

Hello, Sam, it said. I'm a bad memory come to haunt you.......Go away, memory, you make me too sad.....Uh-uh, Sam. You asked to remember everything. I'm just doing my job.

When we made love that afternoon in early October, there were dark, ugly bruises on Jennifer's body. I began to ask her about them but she stopped me and said, "You mustn't ask, Sam. If I talk about it, the magic will go away and we'll never be the same."

I remember just lying there with her, stunned, wanting to say something or do something, but not being able to. I wanted to hurt somebody very much. It surprised me how vengeful I felt.

A little boy walked by and the memory faded. "Are you O.K., mister?" he asked, a concerned look on his little face.

I looked at him and smiled. He couldn't have been more than seven or eight. "Sure son," I said. "I'm O.K...."

He smiled back but continued to look at me in that concerned way that children can have. There's no fooling a child. "If you need me," he said, "just holler. My name's Jeff. What's yours?"

"Sam," I told him. "My name's Sam. Thanks, Jeff."

He walked away and then turned, and waved at me. I missed the dog. He would have made something very philosophical out of the moment. All I could do was to look away and try not to feel the anger that welled up in me whenever I thought of the bruises on Jennifer's body.

"Tell me about it," I asked her later, but she wouldn't and threatened to leave if I persisted.

"No, Sam, just let it go. We're here together, let's make the most of it."

In my heart of hearts, I wanted to track the bastard down and beat him until he couldn't walk. I was astonished at the rage in me, how vile and primitive it was. Had her husband been there that moment, I would have surely killed him. Instead, I got some ice from the machine by the pool and rubbed the bruises and kissed each one to make them better.

Jennifer looked at me and touched my cheek. "There are worse things, Sam, than a beating."

I kissed her lips and shook my head. No, I said silently to myself, no there aren't.

She took me in her arms and pressed me against her breasts as a mother would hug an infant. "Make it better, Sam. Kiss it and make it go away."

And, as if by magic, I did.

Chapter 8

I stood up and walked back down the Narrows Trail to the car. My chest was pounding so hard that I could hear my heart beat. For 4 years I had tried to forget the things that happened to us that fateful year and now they were coming back to me in rushes of memories, as if the floodgates had opened.

I drove to the main lodge in Zion and walked through the gift shop where Jennifer compulsively bought the knick-knacks and assorted souvenirs for friends. I always wondered if this was how she dealt with her guilt, by buying things for friends.

I never said anything. How could I? I was so in love that it would have been like dropping crystal and shattering glass on the ground. That's how fragile she felt to me. In the end, however, it was me who was fragile, who shattered into a million pieces.

There were so many foreign tourists in the lodge that I drove back to the motel and waited for the maids to clean my room. How long would I stay, they asked me when I returned to the motel. "Until I've cleansed my soul," I told them, "until the memories leave me alone."

The dog walked over to me while I waited on the swing for my room to be cleaned. He wanted me to pet him, only mildly interested in my emotional state. If I was any good with animals, I would have made him sit at my feet, wagging his tail, while I told him my sorrows.

There were no foreign tourists 4 years ago when Jen and I were here last. Now they came in busloads. A British lady got off the bus when I was at the lodge, looked around and said, to no one in particular, "Lovely place, this." It could have been a garbage dump for all she knew. Ten minutes in one place, get back in the bus and on to the Grand Canyon, ladies and gents. See America in one day.

Jennifer and I had gone to the "Bit N' Spur" that first time we'd met alone in October. We ate Mexican food, drank tequila shooters, and danced until closing time. Then we made love for the third time that day and fell exhausted into one another's arms.

The stars were out that night, as clear as God could make them, a billion light years away, twinkling and fading like gigantic neon signs in the desert. I love you, said the first one. Oh God, baby, I love you too, said the next one until the stars told our story in some cosmic Morris Code to anyone watching the sky that night.

It was that very night that I first heard Jen cry out in her sleep, a sound so awful it was like an animal crying out or someone dying. "Please, no!" she cried. "Oh, please don't!"

I held her tight until she stopped, my heart pounding like a sledgehammer. I could only imagine the scenes she saw in her mind that night. I felt like a voyeur, an intruder into her private world.

CHAPTER 9

So many of the women I've known since my divorce have been abused by husbands and lovers that it's left a permanent scar on their ability to love another man. I remember a lovely orthodox Jewish woman I saw for a time who told me one night, as we lay in each others arms, her small body shaking in the night from a terrible dream, "I'm afraid all the time. I know he'll do something terrible to me and I don't dare go outside without looking around and seeing if it's safe. I used to be so full of fun and now all I think about is dying."

You wonder why men do such things to women. What could possibly make a loving relationship sour so much? Why would a man become so hateful? I can only guess at the demons my fellow colleagues in the gender wars carry around inside of them for in my family, violence of any kind, except the verbal abuse which we didn't think of as violence, was unthinkable. But in the world of shadows, in the small hurts to the mind and the spirit, the hateful and vindictive words we say can be as harmful as anything we can do to the body because it corrodes and destroys a child's sense of safety. It makes a child long for the good parent to come and rescue him. But, of course, for too many children in our world, the good parent is on extended vacation, hiding out, and the mean and angry parent, the parent capable of doing terribly demeaning things to a child, that parent is the only one the child ever sees. In time, it does awful things to the child's ability to love.

When Jennifer came to Zion with bruises and cried out in the night from the dreams she was having, I wasn't so philosophical about it. I wanted to chase the bastard down and whip him to death. I wanted to vent my rage at the destruction of love. Like a lot of men in our society, Jason believed that beating a wife in a jealous rage was acceptable because real men don't let women take advantage of them. And to make it worse, the friends and family members who help define a man's notion of what's right and wrong, those very men sometimes encourage violence. I don't know. How can men and women love each other with such craziness going on? When will it end?

But I'm starting to sound like a professor of psychology instead of someone deeply in love. Maybe you can never separate the two. Maybe you bring to love the sum total of who you are and what you believe. But it makes me wonder about personal responsibility because we all share the responsibility for violence to children and women. We allow so much violence in our society. We glorify and worship it. We make huge budget movies to pray at its' alter and, at some point, it comes back to haunt us. It just has to end.

CHAPTER 10

I sat alone in my room in Zion, reading an old novel someone had given me, but the words began to collide with one another. I remembered something from the first time we met. Jennifer tore a check from her checkbook with her name, address, and phone number. "Call me when you get to Park City next month, Sam," she said. "Call me or I'll be very hurt."

But I hadn't called her at all. Why not? Fear, perhaps. Disbelief. Guilt that she was married. It all went away when she called me in Park City in early September. "Hi Sam," she said, "remember me?"

Of course I remembered you, Jen, and for the first time in years, the smell of her hair came to me, filling the room with the fragrance of strawberries, and cherries, and lemons.

"God, you smell good," I said one morning when she came out of the shower, her wet hair up in a bun.

"In private, honey, you can call me Jennifer. In public, you can call me God." She said it and let the towel drop, pressing her wet naked body against me. I would truly have called her anything to have her do that again.

I tried to go back to my book, but the words were all melded together. I didn't like what was happening to me and cursed my colleague for convincing me to go on this odyssey of self-discovery. I was used to being numb. I was used to feeling nothing. I didn't like what I was feeling. It felt too much like being alive.

I guess you could call the state that I'd been in a kind of emotional hibernation. I'd been alive and aware, but nothing touched me. I was numb inside. What do you do with a pain so intense that it overwhelms you? I don't know, and I'm a psychologist. Maybe you do what I did. You try and push your feelings so deep inside that they never come out, except sometimes when you think too much, or when you're tired, or when the loneliness makes you feel like death.

I looked out the window of my room. Rain clouds were forming over the canyons. I took a beer from my little cooler. I couldn't remember the last time I'd had a beer. What was happening to me? I was beginning to feel again. It worried me.

One thing that Jennifer said to me that first day when we met in the pool at Zion that I forgot to mention. "I never loved another man until I met you, Sam. I thought I did, but until you love someone so completely it feels like you'll burst, like you're the only one in the world so in love, everything else seems meaningless. That's how I feel about you, Sam. Today, tomorrow, and always."

We were sitting by the pool and she looked into my eyes and said those words to me, that beautiful, serious, sensuous woman. I melted inside. My heart was beating like crazy. I was dizzy in love, intoxicated. That's exactly the way I felt about Jen from that moment on.

She brought a small tape deck with her when we met alone in Zion in early October, and a coffee maker, and bagels, and cream cheese, and every kind of trail mix known to man. We listened to opera at night, wrapped in one other's arms, music so beautiful it made you think that God must have been inside the composer.

I joked about all of the provisions. "Babe," I said, "we're not going on a safari or anything where there isn't any food. We're still here in civilization, even if it is Utah."

She threw herself on me and pinned me to the bed. I couldn't move my body. Nothing worked.

"Of course we're in civilization, even if it is Utah. But who plans to go out, huh? I'm keeping you inside as a sex slave, you big cuddly Jewish professor man," she said, grabbing me in a bear hug and burying her face in my stomach, blowing my flesh with her mouth in what Rachel and I used to call a "Blab."

And then she took my clothes off and I felt powerless. I laid there helpless, and I would give anything to have that experience again.

Later, she made coffee and toasted bagels as if nothing had happened. But I wanted to go outside and howl at the moon like a Coyote in love and beat my chest and holler some primitive Jewish war cry. Not that I knew any, of course, but that's the way I felt.

I looked over at the same bed she'd made love to me on that night and wondered if it had been some sort of fantasy that I'd had about Jen, some sort of middle-age fantasy. Maybe it hadn't happened the way I remembered. Maybe it was just my over-heated Jewish imagination. But the more I remembered of Jen, the more clear and truthful my memories became.

I had to be in North Dakota in three days, long drives each day for me to be there on time. And yet, I couldn't leave. I felt as powerless as I did the night Jen made love to me. I wanted to leave, I wanted to put my thoughts of Jen aside and never think about her again, but I couldn't.

The rain hit the motel window like an explosion. It never rained this time of year in Zion, ever, but it was raining cats and dogs. I looked outside and watched the water pour down the motel driveway. The dog sat under my car, looking at me looking at him. I think he would have come into the room if I'd opened the door for him.

I remembered the second night we were in Zion in October. We were sitting listening to music on her portable machine, drinking wine, I think, or maybe some margaritas I'd made. Jen asked me if I wanted to take Rachel to Zion during Thanksgiving.

"Why?" I asked, thinking that maybe she wanted to meet me here with her son so that we could all be together for the holiday.

"Because," she said, looking at the floor, "I have a little surgery planned for that weekend and I can't use the room I'd reserved. I thought maybe you'd like to use it."

The alarm bells went off in my brain. "What kind of little surgery?" I asked, not sure that I wanted to hear the answer.

She took my hand and placed it on her throat and made me feel the lump on her thyroid. "This kind," she said. "No big deal. Really, Sam, nothing to worry about. It just needs to be done. I'll be fine."

We looked at each other for a moment. "You can't think for a second," I said, "that I'd use your motel room while you were in surgery, do you Jen?"

She shrugged. "I don't want to be a burden," she said.

"We'll be there for you, Jen. Rachel and I, we'll be at your side."

She held me tight. "Somehow I knew you'd say that, Sam. I'm glad."

But I felt sick inside. Sick with grief. My father was right. Never allow yourself to be too happy. Something always comes along and takes it away.

CHAPTER 11

She blew me a kiss the next day as we turned off the road to drive in different directions. No one had done that since I was a child when my mother did it to me at the train station. I was six and embarrassed.

I drove back through the desert, numb. Cancer. She didn't need to say the word. I already knew.

We Jews are curious folks when it comes to illness. We believe in modern medicine, worship the word "doctor," use more medication than anyone can imagine, but deep down inside where we live, where the combined myths of a people have developed over thousands of years, deep down inside we're fatalists when it came to disease. Cancer kills. You could point to the numbers and show us all of the research, you could quote all the scientists in the world who treat cancer, but ask someone Jewish about cancer, and their eyes narrow.

That was how I felt as I drove home through the empty and barren desert on my way back to California. I was heartsick at the thought of Jennifer living with something so unclean inside. In my mind, I could see little parasites eating the life out of her.

She asked me the first time we met what I was looking for in a mate. Of all of the things I said to her, silly and benign and mind-numbingly adolescent, the only thing I remember saying is that I didn't want to be burdened with anyone to take care of. Was it any wonder that she hadn't told me right from the start that she was sick?

When I arrived back in California, there was a message on my machine from Rachel's mom. "Please call, Sam," she said, "it's urgent."

My hands were shaking as I picked up the phone to call Alex. No parent ever makes these calls without a collision of thoughts. It always ends with an accident or an incurable illness.

Alex answered the phone on the first ring. She got down to business right away. "Rachel's in the hospital, Sam. She has diabetes."

I bit the side of my lip. I'd known it for months now, even if the doctor hadn't. I'd seen all of the telltale signs: fatigue, irritability, weight loss, frequent use of the bathroom, unquenchable thirst. Alex didn't believe me at first. I wanted to tell her now that I'd told her so and to say something very mean and cutting to make her feel as awful as I felt, but I didn't. I knew that her heart was as broken as mine.

"You should come down, Sam, she's very frightened."

"Of course," I said, "on the first flight I can get."

We talked for awhile about the details, but I was too numb and anxious to hear anything she said.

I put the phone down and made myself a stiff drink. Then I called Rachel at the hospital. When she started crying and talking about all the needles and the pain she was in, I choked up and I couldn't talk for awhile.

"Don't be upset, daddy," she said on the phone, her voice cracking from the strain. "I'm sorry. I'll take care of myself, you'll see."

I gathered whatever strength you have in these moments and told her that I loved her very much and that there wasn't a thing she could have done to prevent the illness. She had taken care of herself better than most kids ever could. I said that I'd see her first thing in the morning and told her not to worry. If you were going to get sick, diabetes was an illness we knew a lot about and there were all kinds of things we could do to keep her healthy.

"I know, daddy," she said. "That's what the doctor's keep saying, but this little girl in my room has leukemia, and she cries all the time, and I'm scared for her and for me, too. Nobody will like me anymore when they find out, and all of the boys will make fun of me and think that I'm weird."

"Oh no, baby," I said, "you mustn't feel that way. No one will think you're anything but wonderful."

"No they won't," she said, her voice quivering. "And the little girl in my room has no hair, daddy, and she hurts all the time from the medicine."

That night I caught the redeye to Chicago and then changed planes for the small town in Iowa where Rachel lived with her mom and step dad. I saw her in the hospital early the next morning. She looked so small and fragile that I could hardly believe it was her. Twelve times in the doctor's office in five months and they never figured out that it was diabetes until I kept putting pressure on Alex to tell the doctor to check her blood sugars. A simple fifty cent test would have told us months earlier that she had the disease and saved us the pain of watching something eating away at her body, not knowing what it was.

How do you explain such things? How can people be so utterly incompetent? I don't know. We live with it so much of the time, we get so used to it that it stops making us angry. But I was angry now. Some doctor had let my child get sick and I wanted him to suffer as much as Rachel was suffering right now.

I spent the day at the hospital and spoke to the doctors on the hospital staff. The offending doctor who'd misdiagnosed Rachel was in the Bahamas playing golf. The doctors were all reassuring and positive. They never spoke of the gangrene, or the blindness, or the kidney problems, or the serious cardio-vascular problems that accompany diabetes. Nor did I want them to break the spell they were casting. I only wanted to hear the good news. The bad news had a life of its own.

Diabetes. The word sounded foreign to my tongue. What it meant in children Rachel's age was that the pancreas, the organ that controls the levels of sugar in the bloodstream, had stopped working. No one knew why. Some people thought that a virus, released by some genetically predetermined code, allowed the body to attack one of its vital organs. When the pancreas failed, the sugar levels in the body ranged from dangerously high to dangerously low. In either case, it was not unusual for diabetics to suffer comas when the blood sugars become erratic.

That's where insulin came in. If you could read your level of sugar in the bloodstream, then you could give corresponding shots of insulin to do for the body what the pancreas could no longer do. As we were to find out, that involved pricking your finger to get a drop of blood, placing the drop of blood on a strip, and then inserting the strip into a small monitor.

What they weren't so quick to tell us was that any attempt to control blood sugars was always dependent upon the level of exercise, the amount of stress you were under, and the strict adherence to a diet that was very low in sugar. If anything went amiss in your calculations for the day, your sugars could go dangerously low and you became disoriented and in danger of passing out. If they were very high over a long period of time, the cells and organs of the body were bombarded by blood so high in sugar content that it could result in damage to vital organs of the body.

The home health nurses came by the hospital and started teaching Rachel how to take her blood sugar readings and to give herself insulin shots. I forced myself to watch her do both, crying inside for the children who suffer and will never know a day, or a night, without the dread of illness overtaking their fragile bodies.

The little girl with leukemia watched in silence, her eyes deadened by the chemo. I had never seen so young a child with such a pained and dejected look on her face. I could only wonder at why God would choose to do such a thing. It was a thought that plagued me many times in the coming months.

Rachel was released from the hospital the next day. In the few months since I had seen her last her face had become hollow and jaundiced looking. For lack of another description, she looked like a child of the Holocaust, her small, fragile body as delicate and thin as a dried out weed blowing aimlessly in the wind. I wanted to see the doctor who had repeatedly missed the obvious signs of diabetes and do something swift and terrible in retribution for his incompetence.

That evening, we went to a restaurant to celebrate her upcoming birthday. They brought out a cake with candles, but she was so weak that she couldn't blow the candles out and she started to cry.

"Could I have a piece of cake, daddy?" she asked, aware, as I was, that she ought not to because of all the sugar.

"Of course, babe. Just like always. Have a piece and take the rest home for your mom and Bob to taste."

She managed a smile, but I could read the pain in her eyes.

The issue of how the boys would handle her diabetes never came up again. She was so beautiful, even at 10 that the boys were crawling all over one another to be close to her.

After Rachel returned to school, Alex had her give a presentation to her class on diabetes. Rachel's concern about being different ended when one of the less bright kids in the class asked Rachel if she could get diabetes. It sounded, the girl told Rachel, so neat and everything.

I called Jen from Iowa to tell her about Rachel.

"Oh, God, baby," she said, "I'm so sorry. Are you O.K.? Both of your ladies are getting sick on you."

What could I say? When God decides to let you have it with both barrels, you don't have a court of last resorts to argue your case. We chatted for a long time about health, and life, and how everything would be O.K. in the end, but I didn't believe a word of it. For me, the people on high who controlled destiny had just given my life a failing grade for the foreseeable future. God had sealed the book of life for the year and my name was in the column entitled, "trouble."

Rachel told me later that Jennifer called her and talked for a long time. She wouldn't say about what. All she said was, "Jennifer and my mom are the nicest people I know, dad." And then, as an after thought she said, "And so are you."

On the flight back to California, I read everything I could find in the hospital library on diabetes. As a parent, you look for something positive. There was plenty to hope for. The research was exciting and everybody spoke of breakthroughs. I wanted to believe it all, every optimistic and positive thing anyone could say, but I didn't believe any of it. But that's the way I am and you don't help a 10 year-old by being a fatalist.

CHAPTER 12

In the weeks to come, I also read everything I could find about thyroid surgery. It was pretty confusing. I could imagine what Jen was going through having to depend on doctors for her information. Every doctor I'd known in my life had, as their first language, an extreme form of gibberish.

We talked every day. She was being brave and upbeat, but if you listened carefully, you could sense her fear.

What it amounted to was that they couldn't tell if the tumor was benign or malignant until the surgery was done. The million dollar machines and the lab work could not determine, for certain, if the tumor was cancerous, which meant that the thyroid would have to be removed. If the tumor was benign, you lived on thyroid supplements for the rest of your life and thanked God that you'd beaten the cancer.

If the tumor was malignant, you drank a radioactive liquid. The radiation killed the small, remaining part of the thyroid which surgery inevitably left behind. Since the cancer was, in theory, caused by the defective thyroid gland, hopefully the cancer would die when the thyroid died. The thyroid supplement was your substitution for the real thing. They would always need to be modified since the body had a mind of its own and you could never be sure how the supplements would be metabolized by the system.

If, the cancer hadn't spread to the lungs or to the bone-marrow. That was the key. That would be determined be taking a radioactive swallow and then a series of x-rays when the thyroid had been off supplements for at least a month, which meant that a thyroid patient had to endure the physical and emotional fluctuations of a body deprived of the hormones produced by the thyroid. Modern medicine.

Which is what I'd said to my father during one of our many fights over what I would do with myself when I grew up.

"Modern medicine," I'd said. "It's a bunch of witch doctors doing voodoo."

"But it's voodoo that pays well," my pragmatic Russian Jewish father responded.

It precipitated one of our thunderous fights which left him unwilling to talk to me for several gloriously quiet weeks. For my father, it was an act of will not to talk, he loved the sound of his voice so much.

Jennifer called me late one night in October when I was deep into a dream about man-eating parasites of the Amazon. It took four or five rings to wake me up.

"Sam, honey, did I wake you?"

I looked at the clock. Two A.M.

"Are you O.K., babe?" I asked, trying to shake the sleep from my head.

"I lost my voice in class today, Sam. I couldn't talk at all. The students sat there smirking at me. It was just awful. And then they started to talk and to act up. There wasn't a thing I could do to stop them. Oh, Sam, what am I going to do?"

I sat up in bed, very still. Her voice was barely a whisper. I could hear the Santa Anna winds blowing in the background and the house making the noises it made when the high winds hit. It seemed like an omen.

"Sam, are you there?"

"I'm here, baby, I'm always here for you," I said, but the fright was so deep inside me that my hand shook and I had to hold the phone with both hands.

"I saw the surgeon today," she said. "He says that the tumor may have grown around my vocal cords. Even if the tumor's benign, I may not be able to talk again if they sever the vocal cords."

She started to weep on the phone. "Oh, God, Oh, God," she kept saying, "what'll I do then, Sam? I won't be able to teach anymore. Oh, dear God, how will I support myself and Ryan?"

Her words came out breathless, hardly more than a whisper. I wanted to fly to Utah that very second.

"I want to come see you, Jen," I said. "Today. As soon as I can get a flight."

"No, no…I'm a mess, Sam," she said. "I don't want you to see me this way."

I should have gone down that day, regardless of what she said. I should have gone to her work and taken her to lunch, and kissed her hand, and comforted her instead of listening to her frightened voice on the phone. I should have, but I didn't.

Sitting in my room in Zion, I wondered why I hadn't flown up to see her when she called. Maybe, because I'd heard the sound of death in her voice, and it frightened me.

I looked at the wall for a long time, shaking my head in denial. I didn't want to believe that was why, but the thought hung over my head like a black cloud and I sat for a long time feeling troubled and very sad.

I looked out the window of the motel room and saw that the rain had stopped. The sky still looked mean and threatening. Hunger and anxiety drove me from my room and I went back to the "Bit N' Spur" to try on my wings at resolving painful memories and other sorrows.

I sat on the deck across from a pretty Asian lady and her two attractive children. The three of them joked and laughed and I wanted to surround myself, immerse myself in their joy. A happy family, I thought. I watched them and I began to feel lonely for my daughter who could always improve my mood in that magical way of hers. And then a man joined the pretty Asian lady and everything changed. The children became reticent and fidgety and the Asian lady looked over at me. I could see a look of resignation on her face. Her eyes asked me to help her but all I could do was sit and share her sadness. I wanted to tell her to walk away from her pain and get on with her life. If she didn't, then she'd end up just like me; sad and alone, another lonely meal your only prospect for the future.

I watched the man and listened to him brag about some small thing he was doing that had made him late. He was completely oblivious to how wretched everyone else was feeling.

I picked up my drink and sat at another table far enough away that I couldn't see the lady and her unhappy children. Why had I suddenly become so self-righteous, I wondered?

I don't know. Maybe I'd seen myself in the man. Maybe I remembered the same conversation with Alex and Rachel when she was a child. There is nothing more self-absorbed, more incapable of sensitivity to others than a man obsessively into the early stages of his career. Or maybe I just didn't want the sanctity of Zion to be ruined by someone else's unhappiness.

Jennifer lost her voice while she was talking to me that night in late October. She lost it completely. I could barely make out what she said before we said goodbye. But what she said was, "Sam, I need you. Not just now, but for always."

I sat in my bed after she said goodbye and felt overwhelmed with grief. My religious brother had given me a book of Psalms at some point in his attempt to convert me. I found the book and read the Psalm he had suggested when he found out about Rachel and Jennifer. It went:

> The lord is my shepherd, I shall not want. He maketh me to lie down in green pastures: he leadeth me beside the still water. He restoreth my soul: he leadeth me in the paths of righteousness for his name sake. Yea, though I walk in the valley of the shadow of death, I will fear no evil: for thou art with me; thy rod and thy staff they comfort me. Thou preparest a table before me in the presence of mine enemies: thou annointest my head with oil: my cup runneth over. Surely goodness and mercy shall follow me all the days of my life and I will dwell in the house of the lord forever.

Later, in the early morning dawn, I wrote Jen a poem and mailed it so that she would have it as soon as possible. It said:

I walked with you in the desert, my beloved,
and climbed mountains as high as the sky.
I kissed you in the early morning,
and told you of my love,
when it felt so sweet and new
that I became a child again.

I will not let you hurt or cry, my beloved.
Or walk alone in life.
I touch you now, as I touched you when we met,
sweet Jennifer, my life.

And I sent her my "Mezuzah" for luck, my medal with the "Shma'" prayer inside. In Hebrew it began, *"S'hma Yisrael, adonoi elohanu, adoini echod......"* Hear! Oh Israel, the Lord is our God, the Lord is one." I asked her to wear it for luck and to feel my nearness to her.

And then I called Rachel and told her that I loved her with all my heart and soul, and I read her the Twenty-Third Psalm, and we were both transported back in time and saw King David writing the psalm somewhere alone, perhaps in a place like Zion, because it was so incredibly beautiful and full of grace.

CHAPTER 13

We met in Zion in early November, just weeks before her surgery. She was radiant and more beautiful than ever. And optimistic. Her voice had improved and she had that sudden burst of energy the medical books describe in advanced thyroid problems and caution not to take as an indication of improvement in her condition.

That weekend we hiked, made love, danced, spoke of the future, and walked hand in hand through town. It was a wonderful few days. For a moment, I let go of my Jewish fatalism and began to think that the future would be good to us. Jennifer even spoke of moving to California and working at a high school near my home.

We did the strenuous climb up Angel's Landing and walked the last eight hundred yards across a part of the climb less than four feet wide and thousands of feet high over the Valley of Zion. At the bottom of the valley, so tiny it looked like a small sliver in the sun, we could see the Virgin River curving its way across the narrow valley of the Zion. Never have I felt closer to the magic of the universe. We held each other tight, in that moment of splendor, and felt God's presence. Our hearts were beating like crazy from the sheer exhilaration of the climb and the view below us.

While we were still in bed that morning, I told her that we ought not to do a climb so strenuous, but Jennifer laughed, and hugged me, and told me that she already had a mother.

"Don't worry about me, Sam," she said. "Let's have fun and forget the surgery. I have. Come on now, you eternally serious Jewish man, let's get out of ourselves and enjoy the world. 'Outside, Outside myself,'" she said, reciting an ee cummings' poem I knew well, 'there is a world.' Get it?"

I tackled her and pinned her to the bed. We were still half asleep and she was taken by surprise.

"I get it, you little poop. I wrote that damn poem," I said, pulling her under the covers and touching her in the ticklish spots which made her easy prey for a dirt old man with evil intent.

"No! no!" she screamed, "I give up, stop!" And she laughed and joked on the way to the climb and all the way up and all the way down. She kept calling me e.e. and other names, trying on possible first names for e.e. such as Edgar Ellis and Evian Esther. I reminded her of her ticklish spots, but she kept on, walking too fast for me to catch her on the downhill trek.

When we finished the climb, we went directly to the motel and to the hot tub where we stayed until we felt like wet noodles. The days were becoming increasingly shorter. Before long, dusk had come and with it, the cold, dark evening. We watched the stars begin to twinkle in the sky and saw the moon hang like a giant balloon or a golden circle in space.

When the heat from the hot tub began to make us giddy, we ran back to our room in the sudden cold and made love, our bodies in some sort of fever for each other. It felt, for all I can describe, as if a dam had broken and that everything I had inside of me, all of the love and the accumulated passion I'd stored inside, untouched and unused, that all of it came out in that single, incredible moment.

We held on to each other, not wanting the moment to end, fearful that we would never again have another chance to show our love this way.

It wasn't so much passion as an earthly bond. There are no suitable words to use that can explain what had just happened. It was a culmination of the love we had inside which had been wasted on others we did not truly love.

That weekend we made love so often I worried that she might be weakened by it. If anything, she was more robust and eager than ever, clinging to me when we came together, and whispering, "Oh, Sam, I love you so much."

And then the surgery came, but that was another story, and anyone who has ever been through it themselves, or with a loved one, knows that nothing is ever the same again.

My thoughts came in rushes as I laid in my bed in Zion. I tried to sleep that rainy night in Zion with thunder clapping over the canyons like cannons booming, but the thoughts of our love making in that same empty bed left me feeling unsettled. I tossed and turned, fighting the memories of our love making, but they lingered on through the night and would not let me be.

In the morning the cleaning ladies asked me if my soul was cleansed, but decided not after looking at me. I walked over to a pay phone near the motel office and called North Dakota to tell them that I wasn't feeling well and that I'd be a few days late. Or a few weeks, a few months, or a few years, I thought to myself as I hung up the phone.

After the call I walked several blocks to a cowboy restaurant in Springdale and ordered a small stack of pancakes. I wasn't hungry as much as I was lonely and just wanted to be with people. A German couple was huddled over the menu. "What," I heard them say in German, is a "short stack?" They consulted their dictionary. Obviously no one had thought to translate "short stack" into German. They ended up having eggs instead of taking a chance.

I heard the man say something like, "Small chimney," the closest he could come to "short stack" using the dictionary, I guess. His wife mumbled something about crazy Americans and the things we ate, but my German wasn't precise enough and I throttled an urge to turn around and tell them to stuff a wiener schnitzel where the sun doesn't shine, but I didn't.

Whenever Jen and I ate out, we always ordered the things we'd never eaten before. "Why eat what you know about?" she reasoned. "That makes eating out predictable, and restaurants should be places of adventure."

One night I had sweet breads and told her that maybe caution had its strong points. She laughed and made me eat some of her rocky mountain oysters. I was so naive that I didn't know that rocky mountain oysters were the private parts of a male cow. While I was chewing them, thinking to myself that they were a little, umm…clammy, she told me what I was eating and I spit the food all over our table, coughing and gagging all the while she laughed and cavorted with the other diners. A Jewish cowboy, everyone decided, I would never be.

She was like that. She could make an ordinary event into a spectacle. Doing her hair became an epic adventure with tales of past hairdos that left me giddy with laughter. She'd grab a handful of her beautiful hair, molding it into some outrageous hairdo and say, in a voice to do justice to the most effeminate hair dresser in the world, "You just look so fashionable, darling, you'll just break some poor man's heart. I just don't know if I can let you leave looking so smashing."

The day before we left Zion, on a beautiful day in early November, she took me outside and we watched the sun go down and saw the colors of the sky dance across the horizon. If there was another place on earth with so much beauty, I could not imagine it.

We stood arm and arm around each other's shoulder. Jen looked at me, her blue-green eyes translucent and burning. "Promise me that you will talk to the doctor after my surgery," she said, "promise that you'll tell me exactly what he says, no punches pulled."

I looked over at her, the muscles in her jaw pulled tight across her mouth. "What about Jason?" I asked. "What about him, Jen?"

"Sam, the doctor knows everything. He'll talk to you. He knows about Jason and forbad him from coming to the surgery. I don't know what he said, but Jason won't be there. Just you, Sam. Promise, please?"

And I did, that very moment with the colors of the horizon burning holes in the sky. And if I could have rescinded a promise, made myself give it back immediately, I would have. Because no one who has been with a loved one in surgery can ever forget the awful wait or the dreaded doctor's conference after the surgery. It is something like the Chinese Water Torture, if not worse.

CHAPTER 14

Rachel was still too fragile to join me for Thanksgiving or to be there for Jennifer's surgery. Her blood-sugars, those dreaded words to all diabetics, were all over the place as her Pancreas sputtered and started, sputtered and stopped until, soon, it would die altogether.

I called her every day and gradually, slowly, she began to sound like her old self. She had been ill so long that feeling normal was almost abnormal.

The insulin shots and the finger pricking so that she could measure the level of sugar in her blood were still painfully new to her. But the feeling of health, as the visiting nurses had told us, would be a strong reinforcer for her to take care of herself. And if she didn't....the consequences were too awful to think about.

I drove to Salt Lake City one cold and foggy day to be with Jennifer for her surgery. She had been wonderful on the phone before I left California telling me that the surgery was a piece of cake. The surgeon had told her that she might even be able to go home that same day. All of this good news could not shake the feeling of dread I felt on the long drive to Utah or convince me that things would ever quite be the same. I had grown up with an ill mother and had great respect for the way sickness was a destroyer of happiness.

I worried about everything on the drive up. Things so silly I won't bore you with the details other than to say that there wasn't a Jewish man alive who couldn't obsess with the best of them. Freud said, "If you don't worry a lot, you're obviously not Jewish." Maybe it wasn't Freud. Maybe it was Lila, my very Jewish mother, who said it first.

Mostly I felt sorry for myself and angry at being so self-absorbed: Guilt, anxiety, self-hatred and the need to nurture. Put them all together they spelled, J-MAM: Jewish Middle-Aged Man.

I was to stay with Mollie, Jen's friend from grade school. Someone so special, in Jen's eyes, that I was a little fearful of meeting her. I wondered if I could possibly meet Mollie's expectations of Jen's lover.

Is that what I was? I didn't feel like a lover. I felt like the head wise man at Christmas guided by the Northern Star or some other cosmic force. And what of Jason, he of the husband role who was banned from the surgery?

Jason, I discovered, had left home one night and was on a binge or, maybe, to quote Jennifer, "He's gone to seek counseling from someone he respects: Hannibal Lecter."

I called Jen when I hit town. She gave me directions to Mollie's house and said that she would be there to meet me. My stomach felt like someone had filled it with molten lava.

I drove to an area of Salt Lake City bordered by 13th South and 13th East, that odd numbering system which, to this day, confuses me. It is an area of older, moderately priced homes within an easy drive of the University of Utah.

Jen came to the door, hugged me, released me, looked at me in the light from the porch lamp, and called out to someone, "He's wasting away, Moll. Get out the provisions. The man eats like a bird." And then she hugged me again until it hurt. I stood there holding her in the cold Utah night, shivering in my thin California jacket.

"God, it's good to see you, Sam," she said, and picked up my pitiful little valise in one arm and my hand in the other, and took us both inside to meet Mollie.

Who it turned out was a saint, and who took to me as I took to her, immediately. Her first lover had been Jewish, she explained, so it was only natural that she would like me. Had my mother been to Salt Lake City, I wondered? I'd not heard that sort of logic in a long time.

As beautiful as Jennifer was, that is how plain Mollie looked. As sensuous as Jennifer was, that is how asexual Mollie was. But that was before I knew her. Ah, but the heart and soul, they were special. Mollie glowed. A light came from her eyes, those radiant and loving eyes. Together, they were the two most beautiful women I had ever seen. I stood facing them with my mouth open.

They both looked at me and then at one another. "Is something wrong, Sam?" Jen asked.

I shook my head. "I always look this way in the presence of angels," I said, and then I felt sorry that I'd said it because it sounded so trite. Except that I meant it and they did look like angels.

Looking at them, still shivering from the cold, I was suddenly just so incredibly happy. How could anything happen to Jen with such a wonderful friend? It wasn't possible.

Maybe I was giddy from the drive, or maybe it's Jewish to laugh when things are so serious. I don't know, but we started to tell jokes and, before I knew it, we were laughing hysterically. We sat in Mollie's kitchen and told joke after joke until we could hardly talk from laughing so hard.

They call it gallows humor; the need to laugh when things are at their bleakest. Like the man going to his own hanging who says to the crowd awaiting his execution, "I thought they were kidding when I drank too much and they said that I'd have a hangover in the morning."

Anyway, there we sat in Mollie's kitchen eating cheese and crackers and drinking wine, laughing and saying silly and crazy things until, in time, the energy left us and we were forced to face reality. Jennifer was having surgery in the morning and no amount of laughing could ever change that.

Finally, Jennifer looked at her watch and said that it was time for bed. Five o'clock would come sooner than we thought. She took my hand and led me to our room. I remember that it was cold and dark and that Jennifer would not turn the light on. And then she began to cry. Not a hard, intense cry, but a mournful cry full of despair and sorrow.

"If anything happens, Sam," she said between her tears, holding me so hard that I could barely breathe, "I have everything written down. Where I'm to be buried, where Ryan will go, who to call and tell personally."

"Don't, Jen," I said, but she put her hand over my mouth and went on.

"You'll take me to the hospital, please. Please be there when I come out of surgery and tell me as much as you know, Sam, just like you promised."

I held her and told her that I would. We stood there rocking back and forth in the dark, her crying soft and muffled against my chest.

"I'm going to die, Sam," she said. "I had a dream, and in the dream I was watching you climb Angel's Landing. You were alone and tears were falling from your face."

"Don't say that, Jen," I said, but she held me in the dark room and went on.

"I left an envelope for you on the night stand next to our bed," she said. "Please read it if anything goes wrong with the surgery. I love you so much, baby,

I wish we could have had more time together." I could taste her tears in the cold, dark room.

"When this is over, Sam, I want to take you rafting down the Colorado. Just the two of us. We'll camp together on the banks and make love along the river. There are wonderful Indian paintings on the cliffs by the river and we'll go exploring like two school kids. As soon as it's warm, I promise. And if I die, baby," she said, hot tears running down her cheek, "then you'll see me in a dream and it will be almost as good."

We undressed in the dark. Her body was hot to the touch and I kept saying, "It'll be alright, Jen, it'll be alright. God wouldn't let us meet like this and then let anything happen."

I could feel her lips on my cheek as we held each other and the soft, gentle sounds of humming as she fell asleep. It sounded to me like the quiet and tender song of a mother rocking her child after a bad dream. She fell asleep in my arms, an uneasy sleep full of moaning and fearful words that went on through the night.

In the early morning, we drove to the hospital. The air was full of icy fog and silvery crystals that lit up against the headlights of my car. They looked, I think now, like confetti in the early morning mist.

"I dreamed I was your wife," she said, before we reached the hospital. "It was so wonderful."

Chapter 15

My room in Zion was beginning to feel like a cell. When the maid came to clean, I went outside and sat on the swing and waited, the dog looking at me from across the fence. When the room was ready the maid motioned for me to come in. I thanked her for her kindness and watched her walk away, her head bent and a sad, dejected look on her face, just the way Jennifer looked as we walked, shivering from the cold, into the hospital that early morning before Thanksgiving.

I didn't want to think of what happened in the hospital, but my mind had other plans and began to walk with me down memory lane.

It was more awful than I wanted to remember. At first it seemed benign and safe, but then they wheeled her away, all in white, her skin looked feverish and red. She had a temperature of 102 degrees. What was it from? No one knew or seemed to care.

I cycled back and forth between the surgical waiting room and the hospital cafeteria. Everything I ate tasted like poison. They said the surgery would last an hour and a half but it had been two hours now. In awhile it was three. I was beside myself with worry.

I found out from the charge nurse that the surgery had been delayed an hour. "Not to worry," she said, "everything is on schedule."

I tried to take her advice, but the worrier in me had better things to do than to be calm. What if the surgery had left her mute, I thought? Could I give this information to someone I so desperately loved? What if the cancer had spread? The awful thoughts pounded away at my brain and my nervous system was on high alert.

In the cafeteria I sat with a man and had yet another cup of awful hospital coffee. He had the same hangdog look I knew I had on my face. "Cancer," he said. "My wife has cancer."

Oh God, I thought, I didn't want to listen to this, but I sat there anyway, drawn in some perverse way to what he was saying. They were removing her breasts, he told me, and she was only 37 years-old. They weren't sure that she'd live long enough to make the surgery worthwhile but you had to grab hold of everyday of life, didn't you. And then he began to cry. "She's so young and beautiful," he said. "I'll never know anyone like her again."

Which is exactly what I was telling myself. If anything happens to Jennifer, I'll never know anyone so wonderful again.

While we sat in the cafeteria making each other morose and anxious, they paged me. I wished the man well and said that maybe things would be better than he thought, but his face told me otherwise. Then I walked quickly back to the surgical unit. My heart was beating so hard it felt like I had a steamroller in my head. The volunteer at the desk directed me to a conference room where I sat and waited for the surgeon.

After a few minutes, a tall athletic looking man dressed in surgical grays walked hesitantly into the room. His eyes looked uncertain and confused and he glanced at the chart he was holding in his hand. "It's Sam, isn't it?" he asked. I nodded. He reached out his hand and we shook hands in the small conference room.

"We can't be certain about the tumor yet," he said. "To the eye, it looks benign, but we've cold sectioned it to be biopsied. The tumor had spread itself around the vocal cord. I can't be absolutely certain, because of the position of the tumor, but I don't think I damaged the cords. If I did, she'll be able to talk, but her voice will be raspy."

My God, I thought, what a business to be in. I continued to listen to the surgeon's expressionless voice and thought how awful it must be to maim people for a living and so matter of factly share the results.

"To the eye, I can't see any evidence of the tumor spreading, but we'll have to do a radiation series to make sure just before she comes in for the radioactive swallow. I know Jennifer's explained that to you. We need to radiate the thyroid to kill any remaining parts of it that may be responsible for the development of the tumor. Because she's going to have to go off her thyroid supplements before we do the treatment, she'll be deprived of the hormones made by the thyroid and subject to fairly strong mood swings."

I nodded my head. I'd read it all before in the medical books.

"I'll call with the biopsy results in two days," he said. "I think she can go home this afternoon if she's taken good care of." He paused for a moment and went on, his face almost empty of emotion.

"This isn't easy for me, Sam. Jason is a friend of mine. I don't countenance what he did. Jennifer is a special woman and she deserves better. Be as good as you can be with her. This may be a long, hard grind for everyone. Thyroid problems have a mind of their own. No one can say for sure how things will go. We hope and we pray for the best, but we never know."

"Be honest with me, doctor," I said. "I have to go tell that special woman what's up. She'll know if I'm lying. Do you have any reservations?"

"When you do five thyroids a week, sometimes ten, you know the difficulties. Utah has a high rate of thyroid cancer. Jennifer has spent a lot of time outdoors. Like many healthy, active outdoor women her age, she's developed thyroid problems. No one knows why. Perhaps it has to do with the high levels of natural radiation found in Utah, but there could be other reasons. We just don't know yet. The University of Utah is starting a huge project to see if there might be family patterns for certain illnesses. Perhaps this is one."

I sat very still and listened.

"The good news is that thyroid problems, if properly treated, are very curable. The data from a number of research studies show that life expectancy for patients who've had thyroid tumors, malignant and benign, is just about the same as for those who have not experienced the illness. The important issue is whether the tumor is malignant and, if so, has the cancer has spread to the other organs of the body."

"What are the probabilities of that having happened in Jennifer?" I asked in a shaky voice.

"I don't think that's the case, but we won't know for a month until we do the radiation series. What I hope it shows is that the tumor, if it is malignant, is confined to the thyroid. If that's the case, the radiation swallow should kill the remaining malignancy."

"And if it's spread?" I asked, reluctantly, not quite sure I wanted to know.

"Then, Sam, she goes through the treatments that modern medicine has devised to poison the system and to hopefully force the immune system to fight the malignancy. We go to chemotherapy. If that doesn't work, we might use surgery to remove any cancerous tissues before they spread. We just won't know until the radiation series is done."

We looked at one another. His face was as empty as a Chinese Death Mask. There was a long uncomfortable silence and then he said, "I've known Jennifer a long time. Without hope, she'll give up. Tell her the obvious. Keep the speculation to yourself. That's what I would do."

He got up to leave and then turned and looked back at me.

"Perhaps it's none of my business," he said, "and, maybe you already know, but Jason has incurable cirrhosis of the liver, probably from years of excess drinking. I wouldn't predict how long he'll live, but it won't be very long. There are other issues to consider in this relationship you have with Jennifer besides her thyroid problems." And then he stepped outside the door and walked off.

I sat in the little conference room, more like a cell, really, and felt as if my life had been taken from me. I could not move and just sat there with my head in my hands, moaning quietly to myself. Oh, Jen, I kept thinking, please be all right. If you are, I'll be good and I'll be special. I said it to myself but I really said it for God to hear.

I sat that way for so long that I didn't notice the nurse at the door come to fetch me so that I could meet Jennifer when she left the recovery room.

Back in Zion I thought about the scene with the doctor. I should have fixed him with a killer stare and told him that his concern about my ability to deal with Jennifer was none of his business. I should have but, in truth, I said nothing. All I did was watch him leave and wish to God that Jen and I had a magic carpet and that we could go back to California where people were so absolutely, correctly, oblivious to your personal life that no one would ever intrude the way the surgeon had.

I sat in my room in Zion in a kind of stupor, trying to get my thoughts straight about what I'd said to Jennifer when she returned from the recovery room. My mind was more cluttered than I can describe.

Psychologists know that people tend to remember past events in a way that makes them seem, in the light of time, admirable and heroic, which is to say that we lie to ourselves about our past behavior. We become, in our minds, mythical figures full of heroism and grace.

The German Philosopher Nietzsche said something like, "Pride and memory had an argument about what had taken place. Pride, of course, won."

I sat for awhile letting the memories come back, hearing the words as they were spoken, remembering the smells and the sights and sounds of the hospital as they were, not as I would have wished them to be.

As they brought her down the hall from the recovery room, I walked with her to her room, holding her hand. It was hot and dry as if she'd been lost in the desert and had just wound up here in a hospital in Utah. She had a large white patch over her neck.

"I can talk," she said, right off, her voice raspy and weak. A victory of sorts. Then she looked at me, in that out of focus way of hers, waiting for the rest of the story. I could not have lied to her if I'd wanted to.

I hugged her very gently and kissed her cheek. "How wonderful it is to see you, baby," I said, and then I told her, as matter of factly, but as gently and humanely as I could, about what the doctor had said, omitting some things which did not directly have to do with her current condition.

"The surgeon thinks the tumor is benign, but they're going to biopsy it to make sure. They'll know in two days. He doesn't think anything has spread but again, they'll know more when they do the radiation series. He said the prognosis was very good. He wasn't absolutely certain about your voice, but now we know about that for sure."

She looked up at me to check and see if I was telling the truth. From years of being a therapist, I guess I was reasonably good at keeping some things to myself. Good or not, Jennifer squeezed my hand and said, so softly that I almost could not hear it, "Thank you baby, thank you for being with me. I love you, Sam," and then she fell back into a deep sleep.

While she slept, I sat in the room watching her slow rhythmic breathing. She didn't see the worried look on my face.

True to his word, the surgeon let her go home later that day and we spent a quiet Thanksgiving together watching parades and football games on T.V. It was a loving time and Jen seemed to be doing so well that we thought we were out of the woods.

The next day the doctor's nurse called to ask Jennifer to come to the office and have the surgeon look at her stitches.

We spent the early part of the day in bed. I'm ashamed to admit that we made love. Ashamed because the poor woman hadn't really recovered yet, and ashamed because it confirms for many people what they think of men; randy little sex maniacs who can barely contain their needs and who force sick women to have sex.

Guilty, your honor, as charged.

The doctor examined the stitches, pronounced his work superb, and then told us the news. The tumor was malignant.

We looked at each other, and then at him, and then at each other again. There was nothing to say or to ask. We knew the drill as well as anybody in the western world. It was a drill I wouldn't put my worst enemy through, let alone someone I loved.

As Jen and I walked out the door of the surgeons office, she looked at the floor and said, "You do everything right. You're a good and loving and kind person, and then this happens. I don't believe in God," she said, "and I will not honor Him anymore."

I was Jewish and I believed in almost nothing. Fatalism, that's what I believed in. And now, love. I believed firmly, passionately in love, but it scared me to hear Jen say that. A bell went off in my head as I remembered what the surgeon said about Jennifer losing hope.

She turned to me, as if she was reading my mind. "Don't worry Sam," she said," we'll make due. But I'll never trust God again, never. This wasn't necessary to take a young woman with a child, in love, and do this terrible thing. No God who really loves and cares about us would have ever done such a terrible thing."

I nodded my head, more in shame and anguish than in agreement. I was mortified at what would happen to Jennifer. And, without question, I was aware of what could happen to us. Few relationships weather a serious medical problem.

I knew this from the statistics I'd read in my field and I knew this from my mother's long illness.

In fact, it was Lila's illness that I was thinking about when Jen was talking about God. Her illness and how all of us in the family began to find it boring and intrusive. In time, ashamed as I am to admit it, we came to think of her as a recluse, someone who had given up on life, and we resented her for it.

Would I resent Jennifer? I looked at her. For the first time since I had known her I saw something different in her eyes. It was fear, abject fear.

That evening she wouldn't let me sit next to her. She didn't want to give me cancer, she said. After a few minutes of painful silence, she went to her room and would not come out for a very long time. When she did come out, she was holding something in her hand.

"Here," she said, and gave me an envelope. "This is what I wrote for you before I went to the hospital. Please read it if anything happens to me, Sam, but not until then. Promise, Sam."

I looked up at her and took the envelope in my hand. It felt cold and sterile to the touch, like a divorce decree, or some terrible legal document that had just ruined your life and was written in language so high-minded that you didn't know what had happened until you'd read it over three or four times.

I held it in my hand, my mouth open and a pained look on my face. "I'm so sorry, baby," she said, touching my cheek, "I'm just so sorry."

I drove back to California later in the week. By then she was back to her old self and we were planning all kinds of trips together.

"It'll be the same, Sam," she said, walking me to the car in her grandmother's old Indian bathrobe. "We'll lick this, babe," she said. "We will."

She blew me a kiss as I pulled away from the house. My heart skipped a beat when she did that.

She stood there in the cold, in her bathrobe and slippers, blowing me kisses and waving like crazy. I wanted to drive back to the house and take her home with me and care for her. I wanted to let her meet my family and my friends and let them know that we were so much in love that it made my heart swell with pride when I was with her.

I didn't drive back to her house, of course. If I had, maybe things would have turned out better.

Back in the present, I walked up the road and had lunch somewhere empty. It was time to give up this little emotional journey I was on. I decided right then and there to get on with my drive to North Dakota. Tomorrow morning, I told myself. I'd spend today seeing some old haunts and then, in the morning, I'd hit the road. Just me and Chevy Joe, my trusty 78 Chevy.

My god, I thought, as I walked back to the motel remembering that day shortly after her surgery when I was leaving for California, it must have been 10 degrees out and the poor woman, right out of surgery and with a big patch over her throat, that beautiful and brave woman was standing in the cold, waving at me like a crazy lady.

It was a terrible old joke that she told me as I was leaving. What she said was, "That surgeon of mine always had the hots for me. I don't know how many times I refused to go out with him in high school because I was dating Jason. I always thought he'd like to have the opportunity to slit my throat for turning him down so often, and now, he has."

Gallows humor. Good stuff. We laughed as I got in the car. It wasn't until I was away from the house and driving mindlessly down the freeway toward California that my hands began to shake so hard that I had to pull the car over.

It would never be the same for us. I knew it, sitting in the car, watching the people speed by. I knew it, and so did Jen.

I couldn't stop thinking about our times in Zion. Would we ever climb Angel's Landing again or make love in our little motel room? The cars drove by in a mindless procession, the slush from the road covering the car windows. It made me think, for some odd reason, of a funeral. I joined the procession and drove on into the early morning, my head full of the sounds of sorrow and my heart asking God for a miracle.

O Lord, God of my salvation,
let my prayer come before you.
incline your ear to my cry.

My soul is full of troubles
my eyes grow dim through sorrow.
Your wrath has swept over me
and surrounds me like a flood.

CHAPTER 16

This was all sounding so terribly sad and, in its' own way, I suppose it was. But it was also so absolutely wonderful.

Like the time Jennifer started talking about my nose. The family nose. A little crooked, O.K.? A little long, maybe. You never mess with a Jewish person about their nose. It's an off-limits subject.

In high school in North Dakota, these girls with perfect little noses would come up to me and say, "Sam, you're neat and nice looking and all, but your nose, Sam, it's just a little large." And then they'd walk away, giggling like crazy.

As if I could do anything about it. As if I'd asked to have a large nose, for heaven's sake. But Jennifer would come up to me and say, in this positively killer Jewish accent which would knock me dead, "So, you attractive Jewish man, you maybe have a few minutes to spend with a fabulous gentile girl? When we're done, maybe I can give you a nose job."

Nice stuff. Anyone else and I'd of decked em.

Another time, same accent.

"I loff your nose, boobeleh. Maybe my uncle Louie, the brain surgeon, can help with a nose job. Chip for you. He'll make your I.Q. go up at the same time. Two for the price of one."

One time we were in a Japanese restaurant in Salt Lake City and Jennifer called the manager over to complain.

"This man isn't bothering me enough," she said. "I expect mild insanity from my dates."

And the crazy manager gave me a lecture on how I had to be a little more unconventional with my dates and pay more attention to their unconscious motivation. That's what he said, in a slightly cockeyed Japanese version of a Jewish accent. I figured they were in on it, but who can know? She was crazy like that. Everyone adored her.

Another time, standing at a cowboy bar somewhere in Colorado, she started talking very loud in this absolutely awful imitation of a French accent. "Monsieur," she said to the cowboy standing next to her," I know at least 1000 positions for ze love making."

The cowboy looked over at her, this tall gorgeous woman and said, a look of genuine wonder on his face," Well, ma'am, that's quite amazing. I guess I only know one position. It's where the man is on top and the woman is on the bottom."

And Jennifer said, with a look of sheer joy on her face, "Eh, bien, Monsieur Cowboy, 1001"

I had been such an incredible bag of wind, such an academic bore for so long, that all the nuttiness and attention was like manna from heaven. And the sex. God in heaven, 45 years-old and I didn't know sex could be so good. Where had I been all this time?

Good question. I'd been in my head writing nonsense for academic journals. I'd taken the scholarly life more seriously than anyone should. I'd been, truth be known, frozen solid as a human being.

Which is exactly what Alex said when she told me she was leaving me.

"Sam," she said, "you're a nice man, but somewhere along the way you froze up. I can't stand it anymore. You never get upset about anything. Nothing bothers you. I think your blood is full of ice."

I won't mention what she said about my lovemaking.

And she was absolutely right. I was frozen emotionally, until Jennifer came along and taught me how to feel. And, oh my God, what a job she did in that respect.

> By the waters of Babylon,
> where we sat down,
> and there we wept,
> when we remembered Zion.

I didn't know that I could weep, but I could, oh, lord, I could. It's what kept me sane during all of those difficult months when she was so ill. That, and Jennifer's sense of humor, and her beauty because, as God is my witness, she was as beautiful as anything I had ever known in my life. Such beauty made me want to thank God on high and praise his glory.

There was the time when we were driving to California at Christmas and we were stopped by a highway patrolman in Utah because someone had seen Jennifer open a bottle of wine and drink some in the car. When we were stopped, Jennifer told the patrolman that she was dying of cancer. If that didn't give her some leeway in life, she told the patrolman, then nothing did. And here she'd been a good Mormon, too, with a name like Young, and all.

The highway patrolman had a very serious look on his face.

"What kind of cancer?" he asked.

"Thyroid," Jennifer said, suddenly alert.

The patrolman looked at the scar on her neck. "My wife just died of thyroid cancer," he said. "It's nothing to joke about, miss."

Jennifer pulled herself out of her slouch, sat straight up in her seat, and looked at him. "Who's joking?" she said. "Not me, I can tell you that. And I'm sorry for your loss. It's a cruel illness."

"Yes, it is. It surely is." He started to walk away then turned around and said, "Please don't drink in the car, miss. You know the law."

That night we went to Zion and sat in the hot tub, even though it was below freezing, and watched the stars twinkle like little jewels. The steam from the hot tub rose straight up in the cold, still air and covered us in mist. We could see the moon over the canyons staring down at us. Once we thought we could hear the cry of a coyote. The cold air was like a loud speaker. Every time I told Jennifer I loved her, the sound seemed to carry for miles. I didn't care. I wanted everyone to know it.

Earlier that day in the car on the way to California, she'd become very quiet after we left the patrolman. Later we saw him at a cafe along the road having coffee. Jennifer went over to him for a few minutes to chat. When she left, the officer had his head in his hands.

"What did you tell him?" I asked.

"I told him that it wasn't an illness with much pain and that he mustn't blame himself," she answered. "I said that more women had thyroid cancer in Utah than anyone could believe and that I knew a few who had died from it. Good, upstanding, moral women who were good wives and mothers. I also apologized for being so flippant with him about my cancer. No one should intentionally hurt another person. And I thanked him for letting us go."

"Why is he crying?" I asked.

"Because he loved his wife very much," she said. "He loved her more than you could love anyone and he can't shake the sadness he feels every night when he goes home. He can't sleep in their bed anymore because it feels so empty.

"I told him to sleep on her side of the bed. That way he wouldn't feel so lonely. A little part of her would be with him if he did. That's when he started to cry, I think, but I can't be sure. I think he was crying before I joined him."

I think back on it all now, sitting here in Zion, and I miss her so much that I would do anything to see her again. I miss the sense of life she brought to everything she touched, especially me.

I asked her once, when we were joking around in bed late one night, why she had chosen me. And you know what she said, that beautiful, smart, incredible woman? She said, "I didn't choose you, Sam, God did. He chose us to be together. We were his messengers. He chose us because He wanted us to have the gifts we couldn't have in our current lives. He told me, Sam," she said. "He told me when I had the surgery."

I held her tight and thought how exquisite she looked in the moonlight, and how God had such terrific taste to have chosen her as his messenger. I told Him so after Jennifer fell asleep.

By the waters of Babylon,
where we sat down
and there we wept,
when we remembered Zion.
Carry us away captivity,
require of us a song.
How can we sing the Lord's song
in a strange land?

CHAPTER 17

While I was going through my experiences with Jennifer, Alex, my ex-wife, was having a crisis of her own. Interestingly enough, she called me for advice.

"Sam," she said, "it's about Bob and me. I think we're going to get a divorce."

"Oh, God, Alex, I'm really sorry. I like Bob a lot. I figured you two were so happy together," I said.

"He's not a very expressive man, Sam. I thought he was, but he's not."

We were silent on the phone for awhile. It felt uncomfortable and strange to be talking to her like this. We hadn't exactly been friends when we parted.

"Maybe you expect too much, Alex," I said, finally.

She thought for awhile. "Maybe I do." After a long silence she said, "I'm sorry about Jennifer, Sam. Rachel thinks the world of her."

And then she started crying on the phone. She told me that she'd been mistaken to let me go and that she should have been more understanding and supportive.

It didn't exactly make me feel like going out and dancing to hear her say that. She'd taken a chunk of my heart with her when she left, and as much of my ego as you could take and still expect a person to get up in the morning and get dressed by himself.

She was Rachel's mother. We'd spent intimate moments together. At some level, at some point in my life, I'd loved her, but it hurt to hear her now.

Not that I hadn't known it all along. Rachel had confirmed it many times. Her mom was still in love with me. The realization made me feel very sad. For both of us, for all of us who did the best we could in a relationship and, when it wasn't enough and the other person left us, suffered a sense of betrayal that took years before we were truly healed.

I listened to her in that morally superior way we humans have when we feel vindicated, and I told her to get some help and to not give up on Bob. I told her that I believed that he was a good man who loved her and, in case she'd forgotten, that was no small thing in this day and age.

Life is so strange some times. Did it take a potentially dying woman to get my ex-wife to admit to me what I had known these past five years since we'd been divorced?

And then, suddenly, it was as if nothing had been said. We talked about Rachel, she wished me a good new year and thanked me for listening, and then she said goodbye.

We live such desperate lives, F. Scott Fitzgerald said, lives of quiet desperation.

CHAPTER 18

I started to pack the car that afternoon. Zion had become oppressive. While I packed and did what I could to forget everything that had happened, the memories kept floating in and out and I couldn't stop them.

She came back to California with me for Christmas, still weak from the surgery. We had as good a time as you could have, knowing that the next few months of your life would be in the hands of strangers.

She got to see my house, to sleep late, and to make us breakfast in bed. All of the things we were unable to do during our brief visits together. If you slept late during those brief moments, you missed out on a part of the day with the person you loved.

For some reason, my memory of Christmas is very vague. We had a nice time, but Jennifer was preoccupied and not well because of the lack of the hormone made by the thyroid. It made her, she said, sluggish and ill tempered.

As I loaded up the car, trying to keep my thoughts of Christmas clear, the dog came back and sat down by the car. He kept giving me that curious look he'd fixed me with since I first saw him. "Take me with you, Sam," the look said.

"Sorry dog," I told him, "too much excess baggage to take you along, although you are a truly wonderful dog and you deserve better."

And then a strange thing happened. The dog jumped into my car and wouldn't come out. He just curled up in the back seat and wouldn't budge.

I walked over to the motel office and asked the manager if he knew whose dog it was. He looked over at my car and shook his head. "Never seen him before," he said, "must be a stray. We get them once in awhile. Lost dogs someone's forgotten when they leave Zion."

I finally managed to get the dog out of the car with an offer of food and a promise that he could come along with me. Definitely strange. Once he jumped out of the car, he just sat there looking at me. His look wasn't so much curious as it was just plain happy. He wagged his tail and rolled over on the grass and licked my hand. Who says that dogs don't understand English?

And then another strange thing happened. The manager came over with a fax message from my secretary in California, forwarded by the folks in North Dakota. It said, simply: "Please call Mollie in Salt Lake City. Urgent." It also gave her telephone number, which was unnecessary, because I knew it by heart.

My heart pounded in my head while I dialed Mollie's number, but there was no answer. I left a message on her answering machine with my number for her to call. I had done the same thing perhaps a hundred times after Jennifer refused to see me anymore.

I stood by the pay phone, talking to the dog, telling him that maybe Jennifer was well now and wanted to see me. But why was Mollie calling, I wondered? Maybe, because Jen was too shy to call herself? No, that didn't sound at all like Jen. I looked at the dog. He looked back at me.

"You'll have to do a whole better than that if you want to travel with me, partner," I told him.

It was a name that stuck. Partner. I hadn't had a partner since Jen.

Suddenly, I was overcome with anxiety. When Jennifer told me she couldn't see me anymore, I called Mollie again, and again, and again. I fell apart in those months after our breakup. The memory of that time in my life was so painful that I wanted to block it out of view, to hide it behind some huge rock and never think about it again.

My head ran like a sprinter toward some terrible conclusion. Jennifer had found someone else. Perhaps she was suing me for some reason. Crazy, nutty thoughts. Maybe she hadn't seen me out of a need to care for her husband and the guilt she felt from having an affair with me.

I had done this same thing four years ago. I'd sat in my chair in California and dragged myself through every possible reason Jen would not see me. Every reason, that is, but the reason she gave me.

"I'm dying, Sam. I can feel it. It's like some foreign thing is inside of me, eating away at my body."

She looked so good, beautiful, in fact. All of the doctor's reports were optimistic that she'd beaten the cancer. I stood there listening to her, shaking my head, not believing what I was hearing.

"I've seen my friends die, Sam, and I've seen the looks of pity on their husband's faces, the looks of revulsion and disgust. I don't want to go through that with you, Sam. I want us to have been perfect in our love."

"Jen, this is me," I pleaded. "I love you. How can you think I would find anything about you disgusting?"

But she was firm about it, as firm as she could be. She would not take my calls, or see me, or answer my letters. I was devastated, destroyed.

Mollie did talk to me once. "Respect her wishes, Sam. She loves you very much. Get on with your life," she said.

What life? Without Jennifer, I had no life.

"Is she well, Mollie? Can you at least tell me that?"

"No, Sam, I'm her friend. I've promised to stay out of it."

I flew to Salt Lake and asked to see her at work. I was sent away. I called her at home, but her son wouldn't take my calls. I wrote loving letters, angry, resentful and hurtful letters, letters by the stack full. They all came back, unread, and sit in a special drawer in my house, a drawer I've set aside for all of the sad documents I've collected in my life: My divorce decree, Rachel's medical report, rejection slips from publishers.

I never look at the letters that I wrote to Jen. The memory of the state I was in when I wrote them is just too painful.

Maybe I had a nervous breakdown in the months after Jen refused to see me. I don't know anymore. My memory of that time is very poor. I know that I couldn't teach and that they put me on medical leave. I know that I went for weeks without washing myself or eating anything of substance, and that I lost weight and looked gaunt and ill. Someone took me to a sanitarium, for awhile, but I don't remember much of that.

We were in Arizona, rafting down the Colorado River in the early summer. It was the rafting trip that Jen had promised before her surgery. Jennifer was done with the chemotherapy and the other procedures that I won't bother you with. She looked well, considering that she'd just come through the truly sadistic things that medical science does to people when they aren't quite sure how to help them.

The cancer had spread. We discovered that in January. Then she went to the hospital, to a special room lined with lead to protect the staff from radiation poisoning and drank the radiated liquid which would destroy her thyroid and, hopefully, stop the spread of the disease. After two days alone in her lead lined room, she went home and sat alone in her house for five days more days. Alone, because she was radioactive and would have injured a child, or a pregnant woman, or her lover, who sat in a motel room in Salt Lake and waited that awful week out, hooked only to Jennifer by the umbilical cord of the telephone.

Chemotherapy, radiation, and all of the other drugs followed and the awful sickness that went along with them. I flew back and forth to Utah, watching in silent dread as they poisoned her until, in April, she was told that the cancer was in remission. She didn't believe it. Not for a second. Repeatedly, she told me for months that the cancer was still there, hiding out, clever and resolute. It would come back and it would kill her, she told me.

She had dreams about the cancer. It was always a tall thin man who looked like Dracula and who followed her at night and frightened her. Sometimes she was a child when he followed her. Sometimes she was his wife or lover. Sometimes she was an innocent victim. But in every dream, the cancer was Dracula.

All I could think when she told me she couldn't see me any longer was that she didn't love me anymore. She had taken me to the Colorado to soften the blow, to set me up for the knife in my heart. Now that she was well, she didn't need me anymore. Here, Sam, here's your bone, your reward for taking care of me all of these months, for not having a life of your own. Thanks, Sam, and have a nice day.

I felt like the world's biggest fool. You take care of someone and then they dump you. Betrayed. It made me crazy.

It was on our last day on the river. Even I could see if I willed myself to, that she wasn't well. But in the moment of truth, when you lie to yourself the most about someone you love, I didn't see it at all. All I saw was how rosy her cheeks looked and how tanned she was from the sun.

We were sitting by our tent on the little stools we'd taken with us. The river was empty except for the few people who rode by in silence, mesmerized by the beauty and silence of the canyon. We were having a cup of coffee and maybe something to eat for breakfast. I can't remember exactly what. She looked up at me and touched my face and said, "I think we can't see each other anymore, Sam."

I remember thinking that she'd said something else, something garbled or unclear. I know that I was smiling when she told me, and then she said it again, only this time I heard it and my heart stopped beating.

We were in this beautiful spot on the river where the cliffs were almost straight up. I remember seeing Indian paintings on the wall of the canyon when she told me she couldn't see me again. They were of men on horses chasing buffalo. I remember thinking that surely there were no buffalo so far south and that buffalo were only on the plains. Odd that such a thought would strike me then or that

I'd remember it so clearly when so many other things were so vague in my mind from that moment on.

She held me in her arms and hugged me. The cancer was alive in her body, she told me, and it would kill her. She just kept saying it to me, over and over again. She kept telling me that she didn't want me to see her die. She said that death was private and that she wanted to have the time to herself to finish the unfinished business in her life.

A blue bird came down and landed on the scrubby tree next to our tent. He stood on the limb of the tree looking at us, beautiful and alert, it seemed to me, to everything we said and did. I remember how deathly still it seemed in the canyon, and how the occasional sound of a bird in the background was as loud as the crack of a gun shot.

The raft stood against the rocks of the canyon. For a moment, I wanted to take a knife and cut it so we wouldn't leave.

"Oh, Sam," she said, holding me so tight I couldn't breathe, "oh, God, Sam. It's the most difficult thing I've ever done. Don't feel badly, baby, it's for the best. We've had such beauty in our life. Let's not replace it with the ugliness of death."

I held onto her for dear life. I couldn't concentrate of anything she was saying. I could only think of losing her and the fact that my heart was breaking.

"Jesus, Jen," I said, my voice cracking, "don't do this to me. You can't do this to me. I love you so much. Don't you know that?"

But she just stood there holding me as we rocked in one another's arms, and she kept saying that she'd made up her mind and that it was for the best.

"You'll see, baby," she said, the tears running down her face and onto mine. "You'll see. It'll all be for the best. You'll have good memories of me and you won't have to spend your time with a dying woman. It'll be for the best," she kept saying, "it'll be for the best."

But it wasn't for the best and I think that I died that moment. My heart continued beating and my legs carried me where my brain told them to take me, but the life passed from my body and my spirit died.

We rode the rapids back to Jacob's Landing. If a wave had swept me from the raft, it would have felt better than I felt in that moment. Had she picked a time to break up with me when the noise of the river would make it impossible for us to talk? I don't know. What I do know is how it feels to have someone put a knife through your heart.

I argued with her on the ride back to Salt Lake. I accused her of having a lover, God help me, and of using me. I did all of the despicable things you do when someone says that they don't want you anymore. I did everything I could think of doing. Everything, that is, but win her back.

I dropped her off at her home. She walked from the car, slowly, as if she was in great pain. And then she turned and blew me a kiss, the same thing she'd done when she was standing out in the cold in her grandmother's bathrobe. She blew me a kiss, walked slowly, deliberately to her house, and I never saw her again.

I slumped over the steering wheel when she left the car, my head accidentally hitting the horn. I jerked from the sound. I sat there for a long, long time. I could see a reflection through the curtains looking out the window at me, but she never left the house.

I don't remember the drive back home or anything about that day, or the next, or the next.

There is pain and then there is pain. You don't hurt, in this lifetime, much more than you do from the pain of being told that you are no longer needed, or that the person whom you love, does not love you.

That is how I felt when Jennifer walked out of my life. I don't believe I have stopped feeling any differently since.

> I can't make you love me if you don't.
> I can't make your heart feel something it won't.
> Here in the night, in these final hours,
> I will lay down my heart till you feel the power,
> but you won't, no, you won't.—Bonnie Rait

Chapter 19

Partner and I sat on a bench on the lawn of the motel shooting the breeze. He had a very nice manner. If you listened closely, he was very good at giving advice. His advice to me was to chill. "Take it cool, Sam," his sad eyes told me. "Mollie will call back." But it didn't stop me from calling her five times.

The manager finally stuck his head out of the motel door and waved at me. Partner and I raced to the motel office.

"Hello?" I said, panting, "Hello?"

There was a pause on the other end waiting, I guess, for me to catch my breath.

"Hi, Sam," Mollie said. "I'm sorry to call you like this, but I had to."

Oh, God. I didn't want to hear this. I steeled myself for the news by clenching my fist and holding my breath. Partner did the same.

"It's Jennifer, Sam. She's passed away."

"Oh, God, Oh, God." I just kept saying it again and again. "Oh, Jesus."

"Sam, the funeral is tomorrow. Jennifer wanted you to come and to say something."

I started weeping, sobbing so badly I couldn't catch my breath. Partner just kept licking my hand. It was all he could do, I guess.

"Sam, can you come down this evening? Maybe we can talk. You can stay at the house with me if you'd like."

I mumbled something on the phone. I don't know what. Jennifer was dead. Oh sweet Jesus, my Jennifer was dead.

Mollie told me that she'd be up as late as she needed to be. "It's a five hour drive, more or less," she said, but I wasn't listening. All I could do was rub Partner's neck and hug him.

"I have a dog," I said, for some strange reason, but I don't think that Mollie heard me.

I looked down at the dog, my hand still wrapped tightly around the telephone.

"You won't hurt me like that, will you, Partner? You won't love me and then die?" I said through my tears. "I couldn't take it if you did."

And then I said to him, I said it straight to his sad eyes, "Don't love anyone too much, Partner. Don't think that you won't have to pay a price, because in this life if you love too hard, if you care too much, if you think that you are so special, then you'll only get hurt if you do."

Partner sat by my side and looked at me, concerned and sorrowful. I only knew one person who could look that same way when she got hurt, and she'd just died.

CHAPTER 20

It's funny what you remember when you have something awful happen in your life. You remember the little things. When Jennifer had her surgery at Thanksgiving, I remember the frost in the air and the bitter Utah cold, but I don't remember the name of the hospital.

I remember the way her nurse looked, but the doctor who was so arrogant and superior, I wouldn't know him if I saw him on the street.

The drive to Salt Lake was like that. I remember how good Partner was in the car, but I have little memory of anything else.

Partner sat in the back seat and slept, except when I seemed on the verge of crying. Then he'd wake up and lick the back of my neck. It was amazing the instincts that dog had.

Jennifer was dead. What would I say at the funeral? That she was in love with life and had it taken from her way too early? That she was a decent and caring person, but that God had done a cruel thing to take her from all of us who loved her? That my life would not be the same without her now that she was gone?

I remembered my mother's funeral. The rabbi said that he'd talked to her friends and family and, to a person, they said that she was wise, loyal, and the best friend anyone could have. Most of all, he said, she had a goodness in her heart that shinned through like a beacon in the night. Lila was, he said, the essence, the definition of what we thought of when we said, "She was a good Jewish woman."

How did he capture her essence so well when he had not known her? I know that I wept for my mother that day and that I came to know that certain rituals are important to us because they bridge the gap between the unknown and our need for order and reason.

But death is not orderly or reasonable. It is, if anything, the most disorderly of all human acts because it takes life and leaves us nothing in return. Nothing but memories and sad nights missing the one who has passed on. To where? I don't know. I can't think that heaven exists. I hope that it does because some people deserve to be there. But, in my heart of hearts, where I live, I don't believe there is such a place.

I believe in God but, for the life of me, I don't know why. I have seen more than my share of human misery and suffering, and I just don't understand why God would be so cruel and let it happen.

I remember Jennifer saying once that she had become a Catholic because it made her feel right with the world. She had no theology or great religious belief. She liked the services because they made her feel in touch with other people and their lives.

In California, over Christmas, she found a small church and took me there for Sunday Mass. It was a poor church with none of the great ornamentation or pomp that I associated with Catholicism. I sat through the service amazed at how good I felt. So good that when Jennifer stopped seeing me, I went to a service to be with other people. Of all of the things that were done to make me feel better during that time, I doubt that anything made me feel more whole than that service.

We sped on, Partner and I, through the early Utah evening on our mission to see Mollie. I looked outside once and saw dark clouds in the distance and wondered if it was raining in Salt Lake. It was the only thing I remembered of the drive, besides Partner.

I drove up to Mollie's house and parked in front. She was standing on the porch and waved at me as I drove up. Before I left the car, I reached inside the glove compartment and took out a worn envelope. It was the envelope Jennifer had given me the day she found out about her cancer. I was not to read it unless she passed away. My hand trembled when I touched it. It was like touching Jennifer.

Mollie seemed the same, although a look of sadness had come over her. We embraced and stood in the doorway of her house holding on to each other while the night bugs flew around her porch light.

Partner walked over to us and licked Mollie's hand. There was something in the moment and Mollie just broke down and cried. We stood there for the longest time holding each other, swaying to some unknown music in a dance.

She led me into the house and we sat in the same chairs we sat in when I first came to her house right before Jennifer's surgery. Without asking, she brought me a sandwich and something to drink, but I was too numb and broken up to eat or drink anything.

She sat on a chair across from me and I could see the redness in her eyes from crying. "I'm so sorry, Sam," she said. "I know you went through hell."

I shrugged, or maybe I sat and looked off into space. All I could think was that it felt wrong for me to be here without Jennifer. I can also remember thinking that the paint over the fireplace was peeling and how neglected and sad the house looked. But then a friend had said the same thing about my house and I could only guess what it had been like these past four years for Mollie.

We sat in silence for a long time before she began to talk.

"I don't accept what Jennifer did," she said. "It was wrong of her. She did it out of love for you and pride. She didn't want you to see her the way she became. She knew other young women with cancer who had died terrible deaths and she didn't want to burden you with it. She thought that you would move on in your life and find someone else. I didn't, but she wasn't one to change her mind once it was made up.

"But not a day went by, Sam, not a moment passed when she didn't think of you or miss you. The days you spent together were always in her heart and she spoke of you as the person who gave her the courage to live."

I looked at her and tried to listen, but I felt empty inside, as if none of this was really happening to me and that it was all a dream. And then Mollie went to her bedroom and came back holding two pictures.

"This one was taken about the time you and Jennifer began seeing one another." I looked at it and saw a beautiful, strong, vivacious woman in the prime of her life.

"And this one," she said, "was taken perhaps two months ago at Zion."

I looked at the second picture and my heart stopped beating for a second. "This couldn't be Jennifer," I said, holding the picture up as if it were some huge joke that Mollie was pulling on me to make the moment worse.

"It is, Sam, I'm afraid, and it's just a picture. In reality, she looked even worse."

The picture I was holding was of an emaciated woman, skinny, bent and haggard. It was a picture of an old woman ready for death. I could see nothing in it to remind me of Jennifer, and I refused to look at it anymore.

"That's why she didn't want you to see her, Sam. I know you think that you would have handled it well, but I've known too many of us who have had the illness, and when it creates this kind of deformity, the ones we love and depend on can be pretty cruel. I think she wanted to save both of you from falling out of love."

I shook my head. "No, Mollie, it wasn't right. It destroyed me. Not knowing how she felt all these years, not knowing what was happening, it just wasn't right."

"Sam, she was a very sick woman. The medication she was on did terrible things to her mind. Have some compassion and remember that she did it out of love and concern for you."

I thought about that for awhile, but I was suddenly furious and I put off answering her to feed Partner, who sat in the corner watching us as if his life depended on it, but he wouldn't eat.

I walked back and sat across from Mollie. "I don't know, Mollie. My head is spinning. You love someone. You come through tough times with them. You're there when they need you and then, like you're a piece of meat, they drop you with no good reason. It just isn't right."

Mollie nodded her head. "I know, Sam," she said, "but what could I do? She was a headstrong person. You couldn't tell her anything."

Partner was eyeing me from his little corner spot. I almost felt as if he was being critical. "And how can I speak at the funeral tomorrow, Mollie? I mean, I've not been a part of her life for four years.

"What can I say about that?"

I picked up the drink Mollie had brought and held it in my hands just to have something to distract me.

"Maybe I can help," Mollie said, "by telling you about the past four years. The basics, since there are some things that I can't tell you because I'm not entirely certain."

Mollie curled up in her chair. I sat there tense and weary from the day and stared at the wall behind Mollie's head.

"As she withdrew from you, Sam, she also withdrew from me," she said. "Not entirely, of course, but in the important ways that define a friendship, she wasn't there any longer. We'd talk and see one another occasionally, but there were long stretches when I didn't see Jen. I haven't been in her home since before the two of you stopped seeing one another. At one point we didn't see each other for over a year. I thought, perhaps, that she was angry at me, but I didn't know over what."

"Why?" I asked.

"Oh, I think for the same reason she withdrew from you. She didn't want to be a burden and she didn't want to be pitied."

I shook my head. "What a shame, what a shame," I said.

Mollie nodded her head. "I can tell you that all of her old friends took her to Zion two months ago to be with her one last time. She was so weak that we literally had to carry her at times. She wanted to climb up Angel's Landing one last time and to look down on the valley. She said that you two had done it a number of times and that the top of the canyon was a place of calm and peace for her.

"We all met at Zion, maybe twenty of her oldest friends, and we camped out and made our meals together, and sang our old songs. All she could talk about was you. She made us promise that you would know when she passed on. She said that she only wanted you to speak at the funeral, that you would know what to say. She said that she had been having dreams about you. You know Jen and her dreams. In her dreams, you were with a dog, a wonderful dog, and that he gave you solace and courage.

"She wanted you to know that she loved you more each day you were apart. The day she left was the most difficult day of her life. She wanted to run out of the house and hug you and comfort you. What she did, she did for reasons you would understand in time, because, she said that you had the gift of seeing into people's hearts.

"The year you two were together was her lifetime. She didn't want to die, but she had spent a year in the kind of love most people never have, and she regretted nothing other than the hurt she caused you. She told me to tell you that she will be in heaven waiting for you. She knew that you didn't believe in heaven but she'd had conversations with God, and it did exist.

I was wiping tears from my eyes as Mollie spoke. I couldn't stop crying and kept wiping my eyes and taking deep breaths.

"She wanted you to know that heaven was more splendid than any place could possibly be on earth, and that she saw the two of you in heaven together. With God," she said, "sharing his tender mercies. But that before you joined her, you had a challenge that would give meaning to your life and make your time on earth wonderful. She had spent the past four years making certain that you would have a legacy of her love which would last until the two of you were together again."

I looked at Mollie, confused, but she just shook her head. "I can't imagine what she meant, but the will is to be read after the funeral, and you and I are to be there. I guess we'll know then."

We looked at each other, bewildered. Then I realized how tired I was and that I just wanted to go to my room and lie down and remember Jen the way she was when I'd seen her in Zion that first time.

I remembered looking up at Jen our first time in Zion and feeling a jolt go right through my body. My God, I remembered saying to myself, I'm in love with this woman and she hasn't said a word to me. And when she spoke, my heart did flip-flops. I was so in love with her that a bomb could have exploded and I would not have flinched.

To this day when my students ask me to speak of love, it is this image that comes to mind. Seeing Jen and knowing, inside, that I would walk across a pit of fire to be with her.

We live in such an impermanent and superficial world. We throw the word "love" around like it means nothing. But love is forever. If it isn't, then it's nothing but a sham and a lie and nobody should ever use that word again. At least around me, if they know what's good for them.

Aw, Jen. I miss you so much already. Why did you have to die? Who will be with me in my life now that you are gone?

I excused myself and walked into the room and laid down on the bed. I closed my eyes and saw Jen naked in the early morning, holding me and humming a song I could not recognize, her breasts pressed against my chest and her hair smelling of roses. The image of Jennifer danced around in my mind and I fell asleep for awhile thinking, when I awoke, that Jennifer would be lying next to me in bed and what Mollie had just told me was all a bad dream. I thought that I could still smell her shampoo on the pillow.

CHAPTER 21

In the night, I dreamt that Jennifer and I were on the river. The raft was in slow motion and we were holding on to one another and laughing like crazy people.

And then the dream changed and Jennifer was standing in front of me leading me up a beautiful trail. It was the trail in Zion leading to the top of Angel's Landing. We stopped for a long while and looked at the valley below. Jennifer pointed at the river snaking its way through the valley. We both smiled because it was so beautiful.

I awoke in the middle of the night. It took me a moment to get myself oriented and then, with a start, I realized that the dream wasn't about Zion. It was about heaven. I had seen it as Jennifer had meant for me to see it. And she was right. It was more sublime than I could have ever imagined.

I remembered what she had told the highway patrolman who missed his wife. I moved over to the side of the bed that Jennifer had slept on and felt her presence. After awhile, I went back to sleep and throughout the night, I felt Jen next to me, content and innocent. It was the most wonderful feeling I can describe.

Partner looked over at me every once in awhile out of the corner of his eyes. Whenever I awoke, he awoke. "Don't worry boy," I said silently. "I'm O.K."

When I said that, he wagged his tail in reply.

I don't know. You lose someone and you deal with your grief. And if you are very lucky, it teaches you something about life. What had I learned? Only that you take a chance when you love. That you can get hurt and that it isn't always easy or smooth.

But what was the alternative? To be safe? To never take a chance or to risk your feelings with another person? I had done that before and it was like a slow, never-ending death.

Jennifer said to me once when we were just getting to know one another, "Don't play at this, Sam. Don't act like you care if you don't. I'll know it, and everything will be ruined."

I didn't know what to say. I'd never mastered love. I couldn't know if I was being honest. My heart was burning for her, but on the outside, I was such a cold and unfeeling man, so unrelentingly rational, that I thought she would not feel the absolute, out of control, bursting, passionate love I felt for her.

What did I know? I'd ruined every relationship I'd ever had. What could make me think that this would be any different?

But it was different, and I became very good at loving. Jennifer told me so. And when she told me, I knew that it was true. And now, having mastered love, of what value was it to me? There was no one in my life to love, nor would there ever be.

I remembered the envelop and took it out of my pocket. My hand shook. For a moment I wanted to put it away and not read what was inside, but I forced myself to read what it said. It was very brief and it was written in Jennifer's distinctive handwriting. It said:

Dear Sam:

When you read this, I will have passed on. Do not fear the night or cry for me. I have loved you with all my heart and all my soul. I take your memory with me to heaven. But I worry so about you and I wonder if you will be well when I am gone. I hope that you find someone, Sam, because we should never be without someone to love. I hope that she is good to you and that she will bring you happiness. Do not cry, Sam. I am calm and filled with love for you. It is a love I feel secure about and know will stay inside your heart. Cry, baby, for the children who will be alone in this life, but do not cry for me. Jennifer.

After I read Jennifer's letter all I could hear in my head was a song I used to sing.

Who will tie your shoes…
and who will glove your hand…
and who will kiss your ruby lips,
when I am gone.

Chapter 22

The day of the funeral I felt anxious and numb. I followed Mollie around like a zombie. I still didn't know what I would say at the funeral. I hoped that the words would come to me as they often did when I was unprepared for class.

We'd had coffee at the house, but we couldn't speak to one another. It was as if everything had been said last night and there was nothing else to say. We had talked, but it would not bring Jennifer back.

We drove to a small Catholic church where relatives and friends were starting to gather. When Mollie and I walked into the church, people became silent.

Mollie introduced me to the priest and we discussed at what point in the service I would give the eulogy. I recognized a few members of her family from the time they had visited Jen in the hospital. We nodded politely to one another.

I listened to the priest conduct the service. I heard the words but I didn't know what they meant. It felt as if my mind had floated away from my body and that I was hanging suspended from the ceiling of the church.

I remember seeing someone dab their eyes when the priest said something very special about Jennifer. I cannot remember for sure what he said or whether it was actually him or my mind that said it. I know that the elements of my eulogy were forming unconsciously in my head and that I could smell the way Jennifer's hair smelled after she washed it when we would sit outside on the lawn at Zion and she'd let the warm air dry her hair.

When it was my turn to speak, I walked to the front of the congregation and stood for a long time, waiting for the words to form themselves.

For a moment I thought I saw Jennifer at the back of the church, smiling at me. She was wearing a long skirt and a dark blue sweater and her hair was braided in a French braid that made her look like a schoolgirl. It was the way I loved to see her the most.

I wanted her to stay forever and never leave. But she did.

After a pause so long that people began to move around in their seats, I began to speak.

"I found out that Jennifer died last night," I said, "and then it was only by chance that Mollie, her dear friend, was able to reach me. I was in Zion where Jennifer and I met five years ago, reliving those serene moments of joy when we were together. Not all of my memories are sweet or dear, for Jennifer left me four years ago and I can't know for certain how her life was during that time. So I'll talk about the Jennifer I remember."

Far away in the city, I could hear the wail of a siren. It grew loud and soft and continued on as if its journey would not end.

"She was generous, and kind, and fun-loving," I continued. "She was intuitive and deeply spiritual. And she was beautiful within and without. She could be headstrong and stubborn, and she eventually got what she wanted, but never have I known anyone so giving or kind.

"I don't know why God took her from us or what meaning it could possibly serve for her to leave us at so young an age. What I do know is that she is in heaven and that we will meet her when our time has come. I will go happily, and I know that I will only mark time until we are together again.

"It's odd to hear myself speak of heaven. Before I knew Jennifer, I would have scoffed at the notion of a special place where people live with God in eternal peace and tranquility. But Jennifer has convinced me that heaven exits. Not just in the mind, but as a real place. I have no doubt that heaven exits or that we will meet again."

I looked at the people in the church and saw her son Ryan for a moment. He looked so much like her, I thought to myself. His sad face stayed with me as I continued to speak.

"Jennifer allowed me to see heaven in a dream. It is a sublime and wondrous place, just as she said it would be. I know that she is there and that she is radiant and content. The time goes by in an instant in heaven and she will not have to wait long for us to be with her.

"We all hope to live long and healthy lives. We pray that we will be spared from pain. We worship God because we think that He will protect us. We believe that if we are good and decent people that we will be spared the sorrow of poor health or early death.

"Jennifer believed all of this and yet she suffered horribly and, in the end, she was taken from us in her youth. And still I know that she is happy and fulfilled because she gave so freely of herself to so many of us.

"Rabbi Akiva, the medieval Jewish scholar whom many people compare to St. Augustine, said that the good person who is taken from us before his time is a reminder of how fragile life can be. We all despair at the loss of our loved one whose life had such meaning to us. And yet, the good person leaves us with the core of their goodness. It is passed on to us and becomes his or her legacy and it touches all of us so that we are the recipients of the sum total of the goodness of that person. It is for that reason that we should not weep or be angry at God for what seems so senseless an act. Rather, we should rejoice that the world is a better place because goodness is a priceless inheritance and we are all the beneficiaries of that legacy.

"I want to embrace all of you for coming today to remember Jennifer. We are all much better for knowing her. If our lives are empty for now with her absence, they will be full once more when we are with her again.

"Until then, I share with you the most important experience of my life. To have loved Jennifer...to have been intimate with her.... to have seen her smile.... to have known her in great stress and pain.... to have witnessed her joy and her sorrow. These are the precious moments of my life for which I thank God.

"I was blessed with a year of her friendship. Some of you have known her for a lifetime. I am envious. But in that year, I achieved a lifetime of joy.

"I will miss you, Jennifer. I will miss you for now. Until we meet again, I love you, Jennifer. I always will."

I walked off the stage to a seat in the front row next to Mollie. She was crying. She put her arms around me and squeezed me very tight. I could not tell what other people were doing or feeling. It didn't really matter.

CHAPTER 23

Mollie and I drove to the cemetery. Partner wouldn't stay in the car and came out and walked with us to the gravesite.

People gathered around the gravesite and waited for the priest to say the prayers before the body was lowered into the ground. I looked up for a moment and saw Jennifer's son. Holding his hand was a lovely little girl of perhaps three or four. She was dressed all in yellow, Jennifer's favorite color.

The priest said his prayers. All of us who wanted to, put dirt on the coffin after it was lowered into the ground. The little girl came to the side of the grave and put a small handful of dirt into the grave. Those of us who were not crying before the little girl came to the grave began crying after.

I watched her, fascinated. There was something familiar about her.

We all stood for awhile watching the grave being filled with dirt. It seemed so final, this act of burying the coffin. I watched until the coffin was covered and then I turned away so that no one could see my tears. I closed my eyes so that the tears would stop, but they wouldn't.

When I opened my eyes, the little girl in yellow was standing in front of me. She looked up at me and, in a very sweet little voice, she asked me my name.

"My name is Sam," I said, brushing the tears from my eyes, "and what's your name?"

She ignored me for a moment and looked over at Partner. "Is that your dog?" she asked.

"Yes," I said, "it is. His name is Partner."

She walked over to the dog and put her little arms around him and hugged him for dear life. I stood transfixed. Partner just sat on his hind legs, the most loving and content look on his face. All the while she hugged him, he licked her little face.

She walked back to me and took my hand. "My mommy said a man called Sam would come for me. She said that he would have a dog with him. A special dog."

I looked at her closely now. My heart began beating like crazy. She looked so much like Jennifer that I could hardly breathe. The same brown hair and coloring and the hint of extraordinary beauty. She was tall for her age. Her cheeks became colored in the sun, just as Jennifer's did.

I looked at her for so long it became embarrassing. She didn't mind. I saw Jennifer in front of me. Her face, her hair, her eyes. Everything except....Oh my God!..., I said to myself...Oh my God! I backed away and looked at her closely. There was no question about it. She looked exactly like Jennifer except for her little nose, her precious little nose.

I could hardly speak. I looked all around, but no one was looking at us. "What is your name, honey," I asked, hardly daring to hear her name. "I think I knew your mommy."

"I know," she said. "you talked at the church, didn't you?"

"Yes. Yes I did."

"It was nice what you said about mommy. My mommy was a nice lady. She was very sick. Now she's in heaven with my Grammy."

"Thank you," I said. "I'm glad that you liked what I said. I loved your mommy very much."

I looked at her again. I didn't want to be wrong. Perhaps it was my imagination? Maybe it was wishful thinking? But, no, it was very real. She had a lovely, precious, beautiful nose.... just like mine.... just like, dear God, everyone in my family.

"My name is Lila Jennifer," she said, in a small, precious little voice, enunciating every word clearly and precisely, just as her mother had. "And your name is Sam. It's a very nice name."

Tears weld up in my eyes. "That's a lovely name, too, Lila. My mother's name was Lila," I said, almost without the strength now to talk.

"I know. That's what mommy told me. She said she liked the name so much because Sam's mommy was called Lila."

And then she called out to the dog. "Come on along, mommy. Sam is here. We can all go home now."

Whatever she meant by that, Partner wagged his tail and walked over to Lila and me. He stood between us and walked along side of us, glued to our legs as if he were a seeing-eye dog. Maybe in a way, he was.

CHAPTER 24

Lila went with me to the reading of the will. No one could pull her away from me. She was like Jennifer that way. Stubborn and headstrong.

I didn't hear much of what was read, I was in such shock.

When they came to the part concerning me, Mollie nudged me to listen.

The lawyer read the will as follows: "To my beloved Sam, I leave our child, Lila Jennifer. Sam is her father and he will have absolute custody of her after my death. He is a kind and decent man with a daughter he has raised who is wonderful and healthy. He is the only one to have custody of our daughter. If he is so inclined, he may wish to permit our daughter to spend time with those people who have been close to me in my life."

Mollie looked at me, stunned. She didn't know, either. Neither did anyone else in the room. We were all stunned. Lila sat there like a little angel. Partner was sitting at her side, a very silly look on his face. Almost, if I didn't know better, like a grin.

The lawyer also had something for me. He handed me a cassette tape with instructions on the box that said, "To be played after the reading of the will. Only by Sam and Lila."

I listened a bit to the rest of the will. Jennifer left Lila and Ryan the bulk of her estate with provisions for Lila that I heard, but did not comprehend.

"Your mommy left us a tape to listen to," I told Lila when the reading of the will had ended. "I'd like to go back to the car and listen to it on the tape deck. And then we'll talk about how we're going to spend the rest of the day."

We walked back to the car, Lila, Partner and me, like we were family. I guess we were family, in a way. I put the tape in the deck and listened to it hiss for a few seconds. And then Jennifer's voice came on and Lila shrieked, "Mommy. It's my mommy."

I became all choked up inside when I heard her voice.

"Sam and Lila," it began, "my two dear ones. I love you both so very, very much.

"You have met your daughter, Sam. She is God's gift to both of us, but particularly to you, Sam. She is the legacy of our life together and of our love.

"I know that it was wrong of me to stop seeing you, Sam, but it was a difficult time for me. I was pregnant with Lila. The doctor told me to have an abortion or the cancer might spread. I couldn't, Sam. I couldn't destroy our child.

"I know you very well, Sam. The dilemma would have been more than you could bear. In the end, you would have made me have an abortion, but you would have lost your future.

"I didn't want to burden you with a dying woman. You are the most emotional person I know, Sam. You would have suffered as much as I did. And trust me, baby, it is a pain that I cannot describe. I will be happy when it is over.

"The few people who knew about Lila thought that Jason was her father, but most of those who were closest to me did not know about Lila until, I suspect, today at the reading of the will. She was my reason for living when the pain became too much. She is special in so many ways, Sam. But you'll discover that as you get to know her. Still, it was wrong. If you love someone enough, nothing should matter. You said that to me in a dream. I should have listened to you.

"I ache because of the pain I caused you, baby. It hurts me beyond measure to know that you were in pain. Please forgive me, darling. I'll make it up to you when we are together again.

"Lila is like you in so many ways. She is gentle and sensitive and has the gift of seeing inside of people: The very things that attracted you to me. Raise her as you raised Rachel. Teach her about the outdoors. And when she is old enough, take her to Zion and let her know the wonder of the place where we met.

"And finally, my beloved, use your gift to write this all down. For Lila and Ryan and for all of my friends and family who felt hurt and forgotten when the illness made me withdraw from everyone. Write it down along with the poetry you wrote for me. Write it to touch people's souls and to make them feel the wonder of love.

"Your gift to me, Sam, was love. My gift in return is my love for you and a legacy of that love. Someone to whom you can pour all the kind and gentle feelings, the goodwill and excitement you have inside, someone whom you can care for and be cared for in return.

"My memory, my soul, my essence will be with you. Not only in our child, but in other ways that you will realize in time. I will always be at your side, beloved. Always….."

Lila and I sat staring at the tape as it ended. We just sat there for a long time, transfixed and humbled. We didn't want the moment to end or to stop listening to Jennifer's voice.

CHAPTER 25

The next few days were a blur of activity as I did what was necessary to have Lila come live with me in California. She was close to Jennifer's son, Ryan, and it was difficult to explain to her that Ryan would live in Utah with Jennifer's sister while she and I lived in California.

Ryan finally broke the impasse by reminding Lila that their mom had wanted it that way. She had told them both, before she died, that Lila was to live with me and both of them had promised.

Ryan also said that he would see her a lot and that I had promised that she could come visit every chance she had. Lila made me promise that we would visit as much as we could. Like Jennifer, a promise to Lila was the equivalent of something cast in stone, a blood oath.

Partner sat listening to our discussions. Every so often when Lila would get obstinate, Partner would make growling noises deep in his throat and Lila would quickly become agreeable.

I'd look over at Partner whenever he did that but his face was absolutely inscrutable. Blank.

We drove around the city so that Lila could see some of the places she loved the most and would miss like the library, and the petting zoo at Hoagle Park, and Trolley Square.

Before we left for California, Lila and I went to her pre-school and said good-bye to all of the children. They were very attentive for such young children.

"Lila is moving to California with her daddy," the teacher said.

"Why?" a little boy asked her from in back of the room.

"Because," Lila said, "my mommy died and is in heaven with my Grammy."

The children became very quiet with the news. Death was a subject they didn't quite understand yet but the words made them fidget and look elsewhere.

"But I have a dog," Lila said, "and his name is Partner. Want to see him?"

Lila turned to the teacher who nodded her head.

I walked back to the car and let Partner out. He ran up ahead of me to the school entrance. When I opened the door, he ran directly to Lila's room leaving me far behind.

When I caught up with him in the room, he was licking the face of all of the children, shaking hands with every one of them while Lila stood in the corner smiling a huge three and a half year-old smile.

When Partner was done shaking hands, he walked up to Lila and stood at her side. Lila looked at everyone for a long moment and then hugged her teacher. When she did, all of the children came rushing up to her to hug her and to say goodbye while Partner and I looked on.

I had a lump in my throat. She was so passionately like Jennifer, so warm and charismatic and loving that I stood watching her and wished with all of my heart that Jennifer were here with us and could see her lovely daughter and be....what was I trying to say....a family together.

We walked from the schoolroom, hand in hand, Lila waiving at the children and smiling a smile of contentment on her small, beautiful face. A smile I had seen so many times before.

Partner walked between us, his tail wagging like crazy. Like Lila and me, he was ready for our new life. He had two people to love him with all of their hearts and souls. And in the life of anyone, that's more than enough.

Chapter 26

We returned to California and our life together was as natural and as easy as it could have been. Lila is a joy. My future, Jennifer said. She was right.

Lila and I go to Zion as often as we can. She may be able to climb Angel's Landing in another year or so. I hope that I'm in good enough shape to climb the trail with her.

I've never needed a baby sitter. Partner takes care of that job.

Oh, yes, I almost forgot. When Lila and I returned from Salt Lake, a message awaited me on my machine.

"Hi, baby," it said. "I miss you so much. I wish I could see you this minute." Then the tape paused for a long while and we thought it might be finished, but it went on.

"I know it's not very long now before I pass on. Dying seems so cruel. It should come immediately and take us away instead of playing with us and never letting us know for sure when the day will come when we pass on from this place to the next.

"I think of you always and I know in my heart of hearts that I will see you in another life. Be good to Lila and always think of the times we had together. They were the best times of my life. In the worst moments, when the pain is more than I can bare, the memories of our times together gives me strength to go on.

"I see you in my dreams, baby. I hear your voice. I feel you next to me. I know your touch by heart. In the night, when I lie in bed and the night sweats come over me, I feel your cool and tender hands on my face, and I am better.

"I must go now. I can see the man coming for me. I am not afraid. I know there is a better life after this one and that I will be with you and Lila and Ryan.

Pray for me, Sam. I can see his face now. It is a kind face. He's reaching out his hand to me, and I…."

The tape went on for awhile, in silence, its hissing sound filling the room. Lila stood there, frozen, hoping, I think, that her mom would say something else, but the hissing noise went on. And then Lila began to sob and Partner came over and put his head on her lap and looked at her with his sad eyes. I began to cry, too, and Lila and I just stood there holding each other, weeping and struggling with our emotions, hoping that Jennifer would say something else, but she never did.

I went to the machine, finally, and shut it off. Lila and I stood there for a long time, tears in our eyes. We couldn't say anything. We were both too upset. But we had been with Jennifer at the end of her life, and in the scheme of things, that is more than most of us can ever hope for. I wish I had been there in person to hold Jennifer's hand, but maybe that would have been an intrusion. I don't know.

When Lila gets lonesome for her mom, we play the tape and listen to it together. In truth, though, it is too upsetting for me, and I try not to hear the words.

I think of Jennifer a great deal. Lila keeps me busy, of course. I have kept Jennifer's wish to let her friends and family see her very often. It is only fair and Lila enjoys the attention. Maybe I get to be a little boring for her. I am, after all, just a middle-aged academic. We can be pretty boring people for a little girl.

We go to see Jennifer grave whenever we visit Salt Lake City. Mollie is a good friend and Jennifer's family has been kind. Partner always goes where we go. If we try to leave him, he cries and Lila gets upset. In truth, so do I.

Whenever we visit Jennifer, we recite a small poem I wrote. Lila, who is bright beyond any expectation I ever had for a child, and who brings joy to my life in ways I cannot describe, knows it by heart. She brings flowers to her mother and then we say the poem together. It goes like this:

> I will go to the river and I will lie in peace.
> And when the sun sets, I will sleep the peaceful sleep
> of a child.
> And when it is dark and night comes,
> I will go from this place to the next.
> And I will be with God, and I will know
> His tender mercies.

Book Two
The City of Eternal Spring

Chapter 1

It had been two years since Jennifer died. My life had settled into a kind of stable and predictable set of patterns, as predictable and as stable as life can be after the great love of your life dies.

Like most of us in our middle years, you never think that love will be kind. You hope that a special love will come into your life, but past experience and the reality born of age suggest that love is for younger people: Those with good reserves of energy and the built-in ability to forget the hurt and the sorrow, and move on with youthful ease.

My love affair with Jennifer was everything you hoped for and everything you dread that love would be. It had highs that set a standard that no one could possibly match, and lows that nearly destroyed me. I am richer for the experience and I never want the love I had with Jennifer to retreat from my memories.

When Jennifer passed away, she left me with our daughter, Lila, a child of such precociousness that she inspires me to get up and to be active everyday, even though the sadness I feel from Jennifer's death is never far away.

I didn't know that I had a daughter until Jennifer's funeral. She was almost four then and she had been prepared by her mother for the man named Sam who would come for her when her mother died. I found out about my daughter in a way so surprising and at such a vulnerable time in my life that it's a miracle I can get on with my life at all.

But I **have** gone on and I've become the mother and the father to my daughter, filling her life with my memories of Jennifer and trying to be as good and as caring as I would have been had Jennifer been here with us.

I was also left with a strange, almost human dog I found, or who had found me, in Zion National Park just after Jennifer passed away.

Together, we take care of one another because there are days when a melancholy comes over me and I can't move from my bed. I lie there and feel lonely for Jennifer, so sad and empty that Lila and Partner come to my room and sit with me in silence.

I got over it, eventually, but without Lila and Partner, I don't think I could have made it. You lose someone you love and you can't go to the store and buy a new love. God controls love and he hasn't been kind to me these past few years.

Little things would upset me. Anything that reminded me of Jennifer and I would feel a great, unyielding sorrow. It was a terrible time.

I am better now, but the feelings I have for Jennifer come back and, when they do, I am as incapable of fighting them as I ever was. They wrap themselves around me like a misty fog and penetrate my defenses, and I am back in Zion where we met for the first time, astonished by her beauty, unable to speak, in love at first sight.

Love is a funny thing. It doesn't pick you rationally. It doesn't walk around the world and choose two people to be blissfully happy. No, it walks by and it sprinkles love seeds on two people who otherwise might not even look at one another. And when they are so possessed, love says, "So long, folks. You're on your own. Try and be nice."

Most of us ruin it because love can be a demon when it wants to be. You fall in love with people who become your worst nightmare. You love them blindly and they don't love you back. It's a gamble. If you win, then you're the happiest person on the face of the earth. But if you lose, God help you.

I listen to music on the way to work some days. A song comes on by Eric Clapton when I least expect it. It is a song about the tragic loss of his son and it reminds me of Jennifer and of the emptiness I feel without her.

In every heart there is a room
A sanctuary safe and strong
To heal the wounds from lovers past
Until a new one comes along

And so it goes, and so it goes
And you're the only one who knows.

It is, after all, just a song. I shouldn't be so touched by it, and yet I am. The heart is fragile. I should remember, I should have learned and still, like all people who have been addicted to love, I miss it so. To not have love must surely be the worst sorrow. I know, I know, and so it goes.

CHAPTER 2

The call came in mid-April from Jean Henry, an old friend and the co-director of Las Hispañas, a language Institute in Cuernavaca Morelos, Mexico. It was a call that would change our lives in the way all things in love and in life happen by chance.

"If you don't fall in love in Cuernavaca, Sam," she said, trying, I suppose, to find some way to my heart so that I would teach a class for her that summer at the language Institute, "then you've become an old and bitter man and you are lost forever."

Jean always did know how to make me feel great when my life was going downhill in a jet plane. I'd known her for 25 years since our days together in graduate school and she could still make me feel the guilt that I'd prepared myself to master all of my life. I believe that she could make God himself feel guilty.

"I don't care about love, Jean," I said, "I care about Lila. We need to do something special this summer. She's getting bored with me. And Partner hides every time he sees me. I think he expects me to lecture him on Freud or practice dog therapy on him. We need some excitement in our lives."

"Well, Señor Sam," she said in that exaggerated Mexican accent she got from growing up in Shaker Heights, Ohio, "thees ees thee place, no?"

And then she told me about the restaurants, and the flowers, and the Institute where Lila could learn Spanish, and about the great condo they would put us in. She said that it would be a good place to put Jennifer behind me and to get on with my life because I was living a sort of life that was more death than life and if I didn't get over it soon, it would destroy me. "That's good, Jean," I said, "don't hold back. Just try and be honest."

It all sounded pretty wonderful, I'll admit, except, and I tell this to you because it is true of so many people, I didn't know with certainty that I *wanted* to put Jennifer behind me. If I *did*, then I'd have to go through another awful, heartbreaking experience, and I wasn't sure that this time it wouldn't kill me.

I don't care how brave or resolute you are, or how many chances you take in life, if you get hurt in love, and I mean *really* hurt, it's never easy to think that love waits for you a second time.

But Jean kept raising the salary and making the housing sound nicer and nicer. The specialized program for Lila to learn Spanish sounded so intriguing that I finally said yes, just to get her off the phone.

Partner would have to be on his own, she said, before we said goodbye. But how different could Mexican dog food be?

In mid-June, my colleagues from the university where I taught psychology came over and helped us pack. They'd become surrogate family for my little girl whom they loved as much as everybody did.

One of my colleagues gave us a bottle of medicine for *tourista*. Another drank the Mexican beer he'd brought as our going away present. "Bottoms up," he kept saying as he drank another beer.

Partner eyed him from the corner. He wasn't happy about people drinking in Lila's presence. Me, he tolerated because he knew that with my Jewish constitution, one beer and I was tipsy. Two and I was comatose.

"Take care of Sam," they kept telling Lila.

Huh? Wasn't it supposed to be the other way around?

"He can get pretty compulsive about his work and forget that there's a world outside," someone said. Jennifer said the same thing when she was alive.

"Outside, outside myself, there is a world." That's what Jennifer said to me one beautiful fall morning when we climbed to the top of Angel's Landing in Zion National Park and saw the Virgin River snake through the canyon like a ribbon of gold. We sat on a rock, ate trail mix, and looked at the valley and thought that it couldn't be more perfect. But we were wrong and the cancer she unknowingly carried with her that day took her from me and ended her life and, in many ways, mine as well.

Lila looked up and smiled. "My daddy is lots of fun," she said. "He tells really funny jokes and talks Spanish to Partner sometimes, don't you daddy?"

"It's true, Lila," I said, "I do talk Spanish to Partner, but not once in two years, not once has he said anything back to me in Spanish. All he ever does is lick my face or hide under the bed. I'm beginning to think that dog would rather have me talk to him about Freud."

And with that, Partner ran and hid under the bed. Everybody laughed. Everyone but Lila who thought that Partner was the reincarnation of her mother and would not countenance anyone treating Partner like a dog. There were moments when I tended to agree with her, but I'll let you decide that on your own.

CHAPTER 3

We drove from our home in California to the Mexican border at Nogales in my old beat up 78 Chevy. I bought the car from my former father-in-law when it hit 100,000 miles. It was still going strong, although I had been warned that in Mexico it would be highly valued and to watch it like a hawk. To me it was just "Chevy Joe," and I knew it would not let anyone steal it from us. I'd seen the movies about cars that were in love with their owners and believed that "Chevy Joe" loved us and would keep us from harms way.

Taking Lila into Mexico had been a breeze. Getting Partner over the border, however, had taken cunning, political pull, and a fifty-dollar bribe.

The border guard spoke of disease and safety regulations, but after he got the money he said that Partner looked pretty healthy and while he couldn't personally sign the license to bring him in, his father-in-law, a vet as luck would have it, could. A few more dollars were exchanged and we were on our way in "Chevy Joe".... legal, sort of happy, and kind of ready for a new start. Enthusiasm like that could build castles.... sand castles.

The drive down to Cuernavaca was more of an experience than I'd anticipated. Every stop was an adventure and the Mexican people were as kind and as hospitable as they could be. And they did love "Chevy Joe" and wanted to buy him, but we smiled and shook our heads and said that he was *familia,* family, the reincarnation of a lost relative. That seemed a good explanation and they walked away saying that it was a truly noble car, but that it rode too high and the springs should be cut.

"What kind of man drives a car that does not have the beautiful dice and the bronzed shoes of his baby for luck?" I heard one man say to his *compadre*, his friend. And the other man answered, "A foolish man."

And then we were in the City of Eternal Spring, a city so lovely that even the tyrant Cortez, the destroyer of Mexico, a man so ignoble that not one statue of his likeness curses the whole of Mexico anymore, had chosen it as his summer home.

Cuernavaca is high in the Mexican mountains only two hours by toll road from Mexico City. It is a city of flowers and music, excellent restaurants, and beautiful shops for the wealthy who keep summer homes in Cuernavaca, far from the smog and congestion of Mexico City. Little changes in Mexico. The Aztec kings summered in Cuernavaca, then the Conquistadors and now, the super rich. They were all of the same barbaric blood.

As one Mexican writer put it: "From the Aztecs we got blood lust. From the Conquistadors we had lust for our women whom they took from us and raped. From the rich we have the worst of the Aztecs and the Conquistadors, for they rape, and pillage, and kill with impunity and they do it in the name of the people."

The Institute put us up in a small, beautiful complex with luxury condominiums not far from the Institute. For those of you who know Cuernavaca, it was a block off Morelos Boulevard Sur and almost directly across the street from the California Cafe and Commercial Mexicana, the huge American style department store and super market.

Our condo was extraordinarily lovely with thick Mexican tiles on the floor and the wonderful Santa Fe furniture so chic in the United States. When we moved in, fruit and a bottle of wine sat on the table in the dining room with a note from Jean: "Welcome Sam, Lila, and Partner. I'll see you this evening and we'll have dinner together. Su Amiga, Jean."

Lila had a room and a bathroom all to herself. I had a large bedroom with a dressing area and a bathroom right off the outside deck with a view of the mountains through the dense tropical greenery surrounding the complex. Right below the deck I could see the swimming pool where Lila would spend an inordinate amount of time. Like her mother, the child was part amphibian. Through the greenery we could see the active volcano that spilled ash and smoke into the valley and sometimes looked as mean and scary as an Aztec Death Mask.

We unpacked and tried to make ourselves comfortable. I believe that your home is your safe haven. You leave it for a strange place and the strange place is never quite right because the feeling of a safe haven doesn't follow you but stays in place. This would be nice for the summer, but it would not be our safe haven and we all silently accepted it.

Later, Jean took us to a pizza place near the Zocolo, the city square in downtown Cuernavaca, called Marco Polo, and we had lovely little chorizo pizzas and drank Negro Modelo Beer. Lila was tired but intrigued. Partner was so tired he just plopped down next to us and slept. Even an offer of pizza couldn't revive him.

"It'll be good, Sam," Jean said as we ate our pizzas. Time had been good to her and she was still the attractive, slim, dark haired beauty she had been in graduate school when I was in love with her and she rejected me so abruptly that it had been a year before I spoke to her again. She turned out to be, not my lover, but the best friend I ever had.

I nodded my head, unenthusiastically.

"Really, Sam, you'll see," she said. "I've lived here for almost twenty years and it's a place of magic."

I'd had magic in my life. Magic to last a lifetime. Magic frightened me. I wanted calm and predictability. I wanted to hide in my safe corner here in Mexico and not feel too strongly, or think too hard, or live life too passionately. I wanted to be in neutral and not have any bumpy roads in my life.

But you couldn't tell that to a woman like Jean who lived life on the edge and took chances that would frighten most of us. She was always in love, always in turmoil, always deceiving someone or being deceived. She knew everybody in Mexico who was important and had had affairs with any number of them.

Jean was liberated. I was still a prisoner of love. Once was plenty for me. Numbness. It wasn't such a bad state to be in when you thought about it.

CHAPTER 4

Outside our condo, the street vendors sold their wares and sometimes we bought wonderful tamales from the tamale man who had a distinctive way of singing the word,: "ta-ma-layyyyyyys." In Mexico you had your own corner to sell on and your own songs. If anyone impinged on your territory, it was a very serious matter and fights sometimes broke out among vendors.

Jean lived in the complex, which was a blessing or a curse, depending on her mood. One constant remained: her never-ending fight with the owner of the complex, La Señora. We never did find out her full name. It was always, La Señora.

Jean, who had lived there for 10 years and who had fights with La Señora almost daily, called her, *La Bruja*, the witch. She was wonderful to us, however, and took to Lila like the women and the men of Mexico take to all children...as if they were their own.

But Partner, that was another story. She hated Partner, chasing him away from the house with a broomstick so that he would hide somewhere in the complex and wouldn't come out until after La Señora went to bed.

"*Pero, pero*," she'd hiss in Spanish, "may you drown in the pool."

Nothing I could say would make her treat Partner any better. All she would say to me was, *"prohibito, señor, prohibito."*

Dogs were not allowed in the complex, even a magical dog. But Partner got his revenge.

La Señora was a born again Christian. Every Friday afternoon she would have a revival meeting out on the deck behind her house. Whenever the gathered started to sing "Onward Christian Soldiers" in Spanish, Partner would run out onto the deck of our condo, directly across from La Señora's, and howl at the top of his lungs.

La Señora would rush over to our place with fire in her eyes screaming at me to control the dog, that God was offended.

What could I say other than to plead with her that God loved dogs, too, and to suggest that she treat Partner with some dignity. A concept, by the way, that left her grumbling about crazy Americans who cared more about dogs than they did about people.

She would point at the sky and clench her fist, but no amount of threats, no matter how much she invoked the name of the Lord could stop Partner from singing "Onward Christian Soldiers" every Friday afternoon.

Finally, La Señora wised up and started to bring Partner scraps of meat. At first, he'd push them away with his nose but later, after a few weeks of Mexican dog food, he'd go for it. The howling, of course, stopped, although he'd still hum along some. I seem to remember that "Onward Christian Soldiers" was always a particular favorite of Jennifer's, but I could be wrong.

Partner would start the night in Lila's room. After she'd fall asleep and after Lila told Partner about her day and said her prayers, he'd slowly walk to my room. In the middle of the night he'd go see if Lila was O.K. and then he'd spend the rest of the night with her. It was an arrangement that began in California after Lila and Partner came to live with me.

Lila, who was tall for her age and so tanned from the sun that she was often mistaken for a native, began wearing Mexican clothes as soon as we arrived. She found a simple white dress and sandals in the Mercado and wore them with one of Jennifer's old necklaces.

Some women are so beautiful that such simplicity only enhances their beauty. As it was with Jennifer, so now it was with her daughter.

We would take the local bus to and from wherever we were going and the town's people would look at Lila and nod to me in appreciation. One elderly lady on the bus said to me in Spanish, "Such beauty is a gift from God, Señor. Help her to use the gift wisely."

Lila took to Spanish immediately. Her Spanish class ran from 9 AM to 1 PM. Within two weeks she had jumped four sections and was now with the more advanced children who'd had Spanish in their schools or whose parents were bi-lingual. People on the street started talking directly to her, completely ignoring me. Given the quality of my Spanish, it was probably best for everyone.

The Mexican people are among the nicest, the most sincere and genuine people I have ever known. They would approach Lila with candy and chewing gum as gifts. She looked like a miniature Madonna that summer, just like her mother who would have been so proud of her daughter had she lived.

I couldn't stop thinking about Jennifer. The older Lila got and the more she looked like her mother, the more I remembered Jennifer and missed her.

Jean tried to interest me in the women of Cuernavaca, some of whom are among the most beautiful women in a country well known for its beautiful women. But I couldn't let go of my memory of Jennifer. Try though I might, her image and her memory still haunted me.

One of my friends in California said, "Get away, it'll be good for you. You'll be able to meet someone and it will help you get over Jennifer."

How little they knew. I would never stop loving Jennifer. Never. No matter how far away I might be, her spirit, her image stayed on in my heart. An old Mexican love song said it best:

> You are the reincarnation of a love so perfect
> that I will never love another,
> not on this earth.
> Do not tempt me with someone else
> I am spoken for.
> Here on earth and in heaven,
> forever.

Of course, my translation is as bad as my Spanish, but I'd sit up after Lila had gone to sleep and listen to that song and all of the plaintive and sad songs of hopeless love in a country that understood sadness and disappointment and had a special gift for the poetry of unrequited love.

Chapter 5

I taught at the Institute in the morning while Lila took Spanish. She loved her classes and had the vanity of the gifted person who masters things so quickly that it's like a finger exercise for them. Getting her to go to class required no coaxing. She adored all of her teachers and loved her classmates about whom she would tell elaborate stories when we had *comida*, our main meal in the afternoon, as is the way in Mexico.

Laticia, our lovely maid, prepared our large afternoon meal for us. It was always something very fresh and new to our palate. "Daddy," Lila would start before we had even begun to eat, "teacher said that I am the best student she has ever had."

I'd cluck like the appreciative parent that I am and then she would tell me anecdotes from her day in class and the wonderful field trips the children in her class would take around the community. I'd remind her to say grace, a habit we got into after her mother died. Today she asked if she could say it in Spanish. What she said was:

"Dear God in heaven with my mommy, please help all of the poor people in Mexico because they are your children too and you shouldn't only be nice to people in California. Mexico is a beautiful place. I think you should come here and see it. Then you'd be real nice to everyone and they would have lots of food and nice houses." I'm translating loosely, of course.

We sat and talked about school and how much she loved Mexico. "I hope you meet a lady, daddy," she said between bites of steak and salsa. It came out of nowhere, really.

"What made you say that?" I asked.

"Because," she said, "I heard the teachers saying that you were such a nice man and you should meet someone in Mexico."

"Oh," I said. "It sounds like Jean has started the matchmakers going." Actually I used the Yiddish word *Yenta,* which is much more descriptive than matchmaker.

Lila looked over at Partner and then at me. She really was an extraordinarily beautiful child with long auburn hair and translucent blue-green eyes, just like her mother. The tropical sun had tanned her skin and made her cheeks glow like raspberries in bloom.

"And because," she said, "mommy told me. Mommy told me one night that she worries about you and that you should be with someone. A nice lady."

I looked over at Lila. Her mother had the gift of pre-cognition, premonitions or visions like this. I had learned to take them quite seriously.

"Oh?" I said. "You saw your mother? Tell me about it."

"Uh-uh," she said between bites of her food. "Mommy made me promise that I wouldn't."

I asked Laticia in Spanish if she would encourage Lila to talk more about her mother but she told me that the conversations between a dead mother and her child were respected in Mexico and that I must not push too hard. Lila agreed. So did Partner who wagged his tail and yawned, as was his tendency when he agreed with someone.

After *comida,* Lila went down to the pool with Partner and swam most of the afternoon. I worked on my lecture for the next morning.

I know that most people think that academics are boring people who teach boring material. Maybe it's true, but university life for me was a truly wonderful way to live and I loved my special area of psychology that was the helping process we call psychotherapy. In other cultures it was called by other names but the techniques and the underlying theory were often the same.

That summer I was teaching a class on different types of therapy and counseling which I thought might be especially well suited for Latino clients. It was a subject that interested me very much but one which required a great deal of work since the literature I was reading was largely in Spanish. My Spanish was, at best, slow and tortured.

The literature was often written by Latino cultural anthropologists studying the miraculous cures reported by the native shaman or medicine men of Central and South America. The cures were extraordinary because they were so similar to our western ways of doing therapy. This fact led some of us to believe that therapy is a universal concept and that there are common elements of therapy that apply to all cultures.

I lost myself in the text of an article about *dichos,* the wise metaphorical sayings that are an important part of Latino culture. *Sentir en el alma,* for example, translates literally as to feel it in your soul, but the real translation means, to be terribly sorry. *Con la cuhara se le queman los frijoles,* translates literally as, even the best cook burns the beans but, in reality, it means that everyone makes mistakes. *No hay mal que por bien no venga,* translates as, there is nothing bad from which good does not come, or, it is a blessing in disguise.

The article I was reading described a very depressed butcher who was released from a mental hospital to visit his family. Before he left, the therapist reminded him of a Latino *dicho* that said that unless you keep your skills sharpened, they lose their usefulness. It was important, the therapist told the butcher, for him to return to his family or he might lose his ability to communicate with those whom he most loved.

The butcher went back home and in his garage found his old butcher knives that were dull and rusted from lack of use. Remembering what the therapist had said, he took the advice literally, sharpened his knives, and immediately experienced the desire to return to work.

The magic of therapy always astonished me. I read on, oblivious to the world. Gradually I realized that Lila was standing in front of me crying.

"What's wrong, baby?" I asked, taking her in my arms and holding her.

She snuggled against my body and buried her face in my chest.

"I miss mommy," she said between her tears. "I wish she could come back and be with us. God wouldn't mind if she came for a visit. He has lots of people in heaven to keep him company."

I held her close and kissed the top of her head, which was wet from the cold water in the pool.

"Baby," I said, holding her away from me so that she could see me speak. "We both miss your mommy a lot. If she could come back and be with us, she would. I'm just sure of that. But we have to get on with our lives and be happy. That's what your mommy wants the most from us."

"I know, daddy," she said, wiping the tears from her eyes, "but I just miss her so much. I just do."

We stood looking at one another for awhile, caught up in the moment, feeling the hopelessness of it all. If I could have, I would have flown to heaven on angel's wings and brought Jennifer back to see her lovely daughter. But, of course, I couldn't do that yet. Heaven would have to wait, and I told Lila just that.

Later, she drew a picture of an angel holding her mother and bringing her down to have dinner with Partner, Lila, and me. We put the picture up on the wall where Lila said that God would be most likely to see it.

Chapter 6

One day early on in our visit to Mexico, Lila, Partner and I took a local bus to the beautiful silver city of Taxco. It is a city the Conquistadors used to fuel the silver mania that supported the cruel and corrupt regimes of Spain and the despots who ruled Mexico for Spain with an iron fist for 300 uninterrupted years.

Ah, but what a city it was. The crown in the jewel they used to call it. Built on the side of a silver mine used by the Aztecs hundreds of years before Cortez, Taxco looks and feels like a Spanish city, which, in a way it is.

We walked down the streets of Taxco stopping periodically to look in the local stores for the incredible bargains the city is famous for. Earrings, necklaces, bracelets, anything made out of silver imaginable.

Lila asked to buy some inexpensive earrings for Millie, her mother's best friend, and something for her teacher last year when she was in kindergarten. I could hardly believe that she was beginning first grade in the fall. We also bought some earrings for La Señora and for Jean. Lovely inexpensive earrings which felt so special to me that I wished Jennifer would have seen Lila pick them out. Perhaps she had.

Lila took pictures of Partner and me with an inexpensive camera I'd bought her in the states before we left. She had a good eye and had taken some interesting pictures at my birthday party in April. There were pictures of me all over the house wearing a silly little hat on my head and cutting a birthday cake that said, "Happy birthday, old man." Friends could be cruel.

We stopped for lunch at a small restaurant with an incredible view of the city and the hills above the city where they still mined the silver. The owner wouldn't let us in at first because of Partner but I insisted that Partner was a sacred dog, part of our religious beliefs, and finally he let us in. He walked away mumbling something about the crazy Americans he had to put up with but Partner didn't mind and stretched out on the floor as tired and in need of a rest as we were. Lila pulled out his favorite cup, filled it with water, and let him quench his thirst.

We sat eating and looking at the view. Lila looked angelic and content sitting there eating a wonderful Mexican sandwich called a *torta,* which was filled with beans and cheese and sometimes ham, and drinking a glass of lemonade. One of the things that Jennifer had instructed me to do with Lila when I had become her father and only parent was to feed her healthy food. Nothing that had chemicals in it or that wasn't natural.

Jennifer had died of a type of cancer that was epidemic in Utah. She thought that the ground water had caused it since it was contaminated by uranium filings from a local mine. For her, what you put into your body and the cleanliness of the air and water were almost religious concerns and I tried not to violate her trust.

We watched the people come and go, many of them Americans or Europeans who very rude and unpleasant to the waiters. I wanted to go and shake every one of them whenever they treated the kind and gentle Mexican help badly.

Lila, observing the bad behavior said, "Those people should have to wait on the Mexican people who wait on them." It was one of the observations Lila made frequently which reminded me of Jennifer. It is precisely what Jennifer would have said. I just nodded and told her that it was a very wise punishment.

After lunch, we walked out in the gentle Taxco air and went from store to store buying more than we needed but believing we were doing what is known in Yiddish as a *Mitzvah*, a good dead. We could afford the goods and the people needed our business.

At one store, I asked an obviously middle-aged lady how much something cost and added, Señora, to indicate her status as either a married or an older woman. She quickly corrected me by insisting that it was, Señorita, and, consequently, that she was an eligible woman. She gave me a huge grin and everyone around us laughed.

Lila didn't quite get the joke, but it was one of the things that endeared Mexican people to me. Their sense of humor and their play on words always left me in stitches.

We sometimes think that Mexicans are inferior people in America because so many of them who come across the border are very poor, but my experiences have always been that they are the nicest, warmest, most giving people I have ever known. Were we Americans a little more like them, America might be a much better place to live.

We rode the bus back on the winding Mexican road singing the corny songs that Lila and Partner loved so much. Songs like, "You are my sunshine" and "I'm looking over a four leaf clover." Some of the people in the bus joined us, many of them singing in Spanish.

I looked over at Lila who was singing at the top of her lungs and who was wearing a bracelet she'd bought for five pesos. She looked happy and I was suddenly filled me with a deep sense of love and pride for my young daughter.

After awhile, she put her arms around me and fell asleep. I wished Jennifer could see her sitting with me in the mountains of Mexico so beautiful in her simple white dress that people starred at me and when I caught their eyes, nodded and smiled in the way Mexican people do when they approve of someone.

I thought of the old Mexican song Jennifer and I used to love so much and which we listened to the first time we made love almost seven years ago. The song went:

> I am a man from the mountains.
> I thank God for the joy he has given me.
> My children are my treasures,
> Jewels in the night that shine
> in my heart
> and are the eyes to my soul.

At least that's how we translated it one night, as we lay together in one another's arms, fresh from making love, happy beyond description. We were in love, so much in love that nothing else could ever matter.

Jennifer said to me, "Sam, if we ever have a child, it will be a child so perfect that we will both feel like we are in God's presence."

I looked down at my sleeping daughter and felt just that way. Partner looked up at me and nodded his head as if he could read my mind. He was wearing a blue bandanna around his neck that Lila had bought him and he looked smashing. I gave his head a big hug and he nuzzled up against me. It was a lovely way to end a wonderful day.

Chapter 7

When Americans think of Mexico, I'm sure that they think of Puerto Vallarta and Acapulco, or the border towns of Tijuana, Nogales and Juarez. But the Mexico we were living in, Cuernavaca, was an older more formal Mexico where the rules of conduct had developed over a long period of time and were slow to change.

In this part of Mexico, relationships and the interactions of life were based on family status, age and gender. The Institute, in its own way, was an example of the rules of conduct of old Mexico.

I felt it most in the small interactions with the young Spanish instructors who would not look at me directly when they spoke to me and who always used the formal pronouns that signified awareness of the differences in social status.

Many of the young women who taught Spanish at the Institute had lived and gone to school in the United States, but here they spoke to me with a deference that made me feel very old.

It was at the Institute, one morning that I met Patrice Gutierez, a wonderfully beautiful and talented woman whom I would get to know well in the coming months.

I was in Jean 's cluttered office one morning when Patrice walked to the door and looked in. "Are you busy, Jean?" she asked in a voice so throaty and sensuous that it sent shivers down my spine just to hear her speak.

I say this now but a feeling of guilt passed through me when Patrice spoke. Jennifer's memory was as clear and strong as ever.

Jean made the introductions and we each said, "*Con Su Permisso,*" which is the Spanish way of saying, "Pleased to meet you."

She stood looking at me. No. That isn't correct. She stood with her hands on her hips and examined me, slowly and methodically. And then, perhaps liking what she saw, she smiled at me, amused.

That is a look I came to know well; the look of amusement that Patrice wore as if everything in life was just a little silly.

Anyway, she stood looking at me, this very amused look on her face, smiling like her face was going to burst and she said to me, in this deep throaty voice that even a man who'd been celibate now for seven years was certain to take notice of, "You are a very lovely man, Señor Sam," she said. "I think maybe that I should get to know you."

Oh boy, I said to myself, but my knees were buckling, I was so nervous in her presence.

I don't know that I can describe her because that first time I saw her it was her aura, her presence that had such an impact on me. But I'll try.

Patrice was tall for a Mexican woman. Perhaps five foot seven. She had long honey blond hair and a lovely full figure. Her eyes were as blue as any I had ever seen. She looked like a mature Grace Kelly and not at all, not one bit Latino.

I learned later from Jean that she was European, the eight or ten percent of the Mexican population who were not Mezzo American, those with Indian with Spanish blood. Her brother Manuel was one of the silent partners of the Institute who helped with the political problems that needed the special influence of a highly placed Mexican whose family had political clout and status.

I didn't know what to say. I tried to talk, but all that I could do was stammer and did, what any man would do who had not been alone with a desirable woman in so long that he'd forgotten what it was like. I excused myself and said that I had to go to class.

"Oh?" she asked in that throaty voice of hers, "you are a teacher at Las Hispañas?

Jean chimed in, sensing my discomfort. "Sam is a very famous author who is teaching a course on the psychotherapy movement in Latin America."

"Oh?" Patrice said, "I should love to attend a class. I am interested in the psychotherapy movement in Latin America," but her smile said that the course sounded like dog poop and only a complete fool would be interested in anything so inane.

I looked at her for a moment, screwed up the courage to talk and said, "Somehow, Ms. Gutierez, I rather think that the subject would bore the pants off of you."

And she replied, "So early in our relationship, Señor, and you are talking about my pants?"

If she hadn't been so beautiful, and if her voice hadn't been so sensuous, and if she hadn't smelled so good, and if I wasn't a gentleman, I'd have had some terrific come back, but I didn't. I just stood there like a fool, unable to think of anything to say, too embarrassed to tell her how she made my blood run hot and too out of practice to small talk my way out of the room with any degree of grace.

Partner, who followed me around everywhere while Lila was in class, looked at me with this absolutely blank look. No help there.

I groveled my way past Patrice Gutierez and out the door of Jean 's office but felt those incredible hot eyes on my back as I left. I don't know for sure, but I think she laughed as I left. A throaty, sensual laugh that left me shivering in the warm tropical air.

I was disturbed and preoccupied all the way through class. I was still in mourning. This just wasn't right, and I vowed that I would have Jean explain my situation to Patrice Gutierez. But all I could think about throughout my discussion of *dichos* was the saying the Italians had about being smitten by a beautiful woman: "Love is like a bolt of lightening. You cannot control where it will hit or keep from getting burned."

Jean wasn't around after class, but all the young Spanish teachers were talking and every so often they would look over at me and giggle.

"What's up?" I would ask them in Spanish, but that made them laugh even more.

I waited for Lila to finish class and then we walked back to our house, perhaps a fifteen-minute walk up Morelos Sur and through the parking lot of Commercial Mexicana.

The walk home sent us by the stores and the discos that are so much a part of Mexican life. Music blared from the discos anytime of day or night and we would sometimes stand and watch the dancers and Lila would try and imitate them.

Some of the homes along our walk were more like mansions, and you realized that Cuernavaca was a very wealthy city when you saw the homes which were so beautiful that you could never dream of living in a place so splendid.

The street was full of honking cars. Many were the old Volkswagen Beetles from the 60's that were now manufactured in Mexico and filled the street with the cars of my youth. You wouldn't want to drive in Mexico because the rules were vague and there was a fearsome price if you inadvertently broke any of them.

The parking lot at Commercial Mexicana was always filled with American cars. A uniformed Mexican guard whistled drivers into parking spots that in America, we would have chosen on our own. But Mexico is a poor country and the guards made their living from the tips they received from the drivers who could afford a peso here and there and who put up with the practice of tipping unnecessary labor because it was a tradition that kept things running in a country as poor as Mexico was.

Lila chattered away about the class and told me all of the new words she knew in Spanish, many of which I didn't know. "*Hola, Papacito,*" she said, showing off what she had learned and then asking me for a kiss on her ear in Spanish.

Laticia had another exquisite meal prepared for us that we ate with relish. For Partner, she fixed dog food and the scraps La Señora gave us plus a little bit of what we were eating. Partner always licked her hand and Laticia seemed to respect Partner's magical qualities. She would say to him in Spanish, "You are so beautiful, *mi amigo,* that I could give you a big smooch."

She never did, of course, but not because Partner didn't want her to.

After we ate, Lila put on her swimsuit and she and Partner went down to the pool. I got out my books to read but the presence of Patrice Gutierez was still with me and I couldn't concentrate.

I sat in the chair thinking about Patrice, guessing that you'd have to be crazy to get involved with anyone so aggressive and arrogant, when Laticia brought me a note she said a young man had brought to the front gate. The note said, "Señor Sam and Señorita Lila. You are cordially invited to a party at the Gutierez home, *Sabido* (Saturday) at eight o'clock." It was signed, Manuel Gutierez with a special note hand written in Spanish that said, "Sam, we are celebrating the twenty-fifth year of the Institute. You would honor us to attend. Some very important people from Mexico City will be there. Your humble servant, Manuel."

Sure, I thought, if this didn't have the imprint of Patrice Gutierez on it, nothing did. But later Jean came over and said that Manuel needed me to be there. Actually, the Institute needed me because some federal politicos were coming to the party because the Institute was applying for a grant to train other Spanish teachers in the techniques used by the Institute to train new students in the language. They needed someone with academic credentials to make the Institute look good.

Jean pulled out a bottle of very good cognac. "A bribe," she said.

I looked over at her tired eyes as she slumped down in my chair, smiled and said, "Accepted."

The issue of Patrice never came up again and I soon forgot about her as I went about my daily chores as an instructor, father, and owner of a magical dog.

I had Partner give La Señora the earrings we had chosen. He carried the package with the earrings in his mouth while Lila knocked on the door, a broad smile on her beautiful little face.

"Here," she said in Spanish, giving La Señora the earrings we had bought in Taxco, "a present from Partner and from me and my daddy. We love you."

La Señora looked down at Lila and gave her a hug. She was wiping tears out of her eyes when I looked over through our kitchen window.

CHAPTER 8

I got on with my life, forgetting Patrice Gutierez and the party on Saturday while I did the many things needed to be done by a parent, dog owner and teacher. One day late in the week the three of us walked to La India Bonita near the Zocolo, the center of the city, and had a wonderful breakfast,

You really could not get an American style breakfast anywhere in Cuernavaca except at the California Cafe across the street from our condo complex. But their food tasted like any number of fast food chains in California and most of the patrons were Americans. We considered the places within walking distance where we could get a good breakfast and opted for La India Bonita, a restaurant tucked away on a side street, largely outdoors, and surely serving the best Huevos Rancheros, eggs with salsa and hot sticky rolls and tortillas, in the entire world.

The restaurant was lush with tropical plants. The chairs and tables were the old, heavy Mexican pieces that were so comfortable you didn't want to get up once you were seated. All around the restaurant you could see plants, and exotic flowers, and original paintings by, I was told, some of the most famous artists in Mexico.

The waitresses loved to joke with us and would say in very formal and exaggerated Spanish as we walked in, "Ah, the North Americans have come to complain about our food again. I suppose the Señor will hate our coffee."

We would assure them that we loved every single thing about their food and would beg and plead for certain extras like a slice of ham with our eggs. The waitresses would raise their eyebrows and give us a look that said they didn't believe us and that what we were asking for was certainly well beyond reason and impossible to provide.

But then they would serve me huge mugs of hot, delicious coffee with the heavy cream you add to your coffee in Mexico instead of milk and the things they weren't supposed to make like French toast for Lila, and we would know that we were still in their good graces.

"I suppose the Señor will complain again about the food to the manager," they would say just in hearing range but we would leave huge tips and come back again and again.

Lila always insisted on saying grace in Spanish and would ask the waitresses to join us, all of whom were religious and were always moved by Lila's prayers. This time she gathered everyone around. She told us to fold our hands and she said:

"*Estimado Señor Christe* (Dear Jesus), we are happy that our friends are here and we thank them for bringing us such wonderful and delicious food. We know that you will treat them all well, and that they will find nice men to marry and have many beautiful children, and that they will be rich and prosper."

All right, so I helped out by writing the prayer. I admit it. But the ladies at La India Bonita would give Lila big kisses after the prayers and bring the incredible cups of hot Mexican chocolate with real whipped cream, and they would not let Lila leave without giving her a candy or two from the special stock the manager said was only for very special guests. We were very special, they reasoned, so it was only right.

Later, we discovered that the restaurant was voted one of the ten best in the entire country by *The New York Times*, but to us it was only a special place to have breakfast.

That morning while we ate breakfast outdoors and the weather blessed us with another day so lovely it would make your heart ache to think of leaving Cuernavaca, Patrice Gutierez walked up to our table and politely asked if she could join us. The waitresses all raised their eyebrows and shook their head in disbelief. I would never live this down.

"How are you, Sam?" she asked in her very good English with just a trace of an accent and her throaty voice that made me shiver in the warm Cuernavaca morning.

"I'm well, Patrice," and I introduced her to Lila and Partner. "And how are you?" I added.

"Well, Sam, I am well. I am sorry to intrude on you like this…"

"It's lovely to see you Patrice," I said. "Please sit and have breakfast with us."

"No, no. Perhaps some coffee."

I pointed to my coffee and then to Patrice and the waitress brought her coffee, but the look on her face said something like, "What is she doing here spoiling our nice morning."

Mexican women, as I was to discover, were very possessive.

I looked over at Patrice. She was even more beautiful in the clear light of morning than I had thought the first time I saw her in Jean's office. She was wearing very high heals, as is the custom in Mexico, a tight long dress with a slit up the side showing lovely legs, and a white silk blouse. You would have to have been a cleric not to notice what was inside the blouse. I did and I was as close to being a cleric as you could get.

"I wanted to apologize, Sam, for the way I was in Jean 's office. She told me about your loss and that you are still in mourning. It was not correct of me to have been so forward."

Lila stopped drinking her chocolate and took a long hard look at Patrice. So, in fact, did Partner, though he seemed more interested in the last sticky bun on the table.

I didn't know what to say. I wasn't sure that I should say anything.

"Although, it is true," she continued, "that I find you very attractive, it would be incorrect of me to continue suggesting that we might meet or get to know one another."

"Why?" I asked, suddenly, out of thin air, a little confused by what I had just said.

The amused smile came back. "Well…"

She didn't finish. She didn't have to.

"You are enjoying your stay in Cuernavaca?" she asked, finally, but all I could think about was the way her lips looked as they formed each word.

"Cuernavaca is the most beautiful place I have ever known," I said, finally, happy to form a complete sentence without feeling like a certifiable idiot.

"Yes, it is. I was born here and have lived here much of my life, but it is still the most beautiful place I have ever known. And your courses," she asked, "they go well?"

I couldn't stop looking at her. *Madre mia!* as they say in Spanish, my heart was going in six directions.

"It goes well but I feel as if I don't really know the subject. My Spanish is still not so great that I can read all of the literature easily."

"If I can help," she said, "please don't hesitate to ask."

I looked at her as she spoke and watched how her eyes sparkled and the way her delicate hands moved and how she would brush an imaginary strand of hair from her face as she spoke. I could not take my eyes off of her, she was so beautiful.

I haven't known many men who are comfortable in the presence of beautiful women. Something about such beauty brings out our insecurities and our innate belief that we couldn't attract a bag lady on the best of days. But with Patrice, in that precise moment, something came over me in her presence: A calm, a feeling of stability, an acceptance, perhaps, and I put to rest my nervousness and sat and spoke to her about many things. We discussed my work, the Institute, and our families. My family sat and looked at their parent speaking to this exceptional woman as if such things happened every day.

Patrice told me stories about Jean and how she could fly off the handle in a wink of an eye that made me laugh so hard that, at one point, I spit up my coffee.

I looked over at the waitresses who had gathered around to gossip about us and watched them shake their heads at my antics. When the lightening bolt hit, I could imagine them saying, the men acted like idiots no matter how smart they were.

Then I looked at my watch and pronounced it time to head back to class. Patrice offered to drive us back but we had a rule that we walked whenever we could because it was good exercise and it let us see more of the city.

We shook hands before we left, which is the custom between men and women in Mexico. I felt her soft delicate hand against mine and for a moment longer then they should have, our hands lingered together. I looked into Patrice's eyes. They were bright, and clear, and lovely. I don't remember seeing the amused look on her face when we left.

We walked back to Morelos Sur from La India Bonita and past the Cathedral and the vendors who always had their products out to sell. The buses ran up Morelos and the people piled on and off. Across the street we saw the sick people going in and out of the hospital and their relatives who shuffled food and supplies in to them since the hospital had neither food nor supplies for the sick people of Cuernavaca.

The sky was a brilliant blue and the trees and flowers all along Morelos Sur were in full bloom. Birds flew from tree to tree and chirped and sang beautiful songs while the shopkeepers washed the dust from the walkways in front of their stores and everyone nodded and said, "*Buenos dias*," good morning.

On the walk to the Institute, Lila suddenly became very whiny and wanted to take a cab. We never took cabs when we could walk, I reminded her, but to no avail. She didn't want to walk and started to get that look in her eyes that suggested the onset of tears.

I took her aside and asked her what was wrong.

"Nothing," she said in that defiant way children talk when they're the most upset.

"Come on, babe, I can't read minds. You have to tell me what's bothering you."

She struggled with words but said, finally, "I don't like that lady. Neither does Partner, and mommy wouldn't like her either."

"Why don't you like her, Lila?" I asked.

"Because she's not nice," Lila said.

I made that look with my face to suggest that I wasn't sure what she meant and Lila said, "She smiles all the time like she's so smart, daddy, and she isn't. Partner and I think she's stuck-up."

Out of the mouths of babes, as they say.

"Well, babe," I said, "I think maybe you're right. But you never know until you get to really know someone, do you?"

Lila shrugged. Partner yawned. There was a lot of heavy-duty non-verbal language going on here.

"You said that I should meet someone. How can I do that without ever going out with them and getting to know them a little?"

"I don't know," Lila said in a very small voice. "I just don't like that Patrice. She smiles too much."

I took Lila in my arms and held her.

"I wish your mom was here in Mexico with us," I said, "and then there would be no Patrice or anyone else. I love your mom so much I'm not sure that I can go out with anyone else again. We just need to keep talking and not get our feelings hurt, O.K.?"

Lila looked up at me. "You won't love Patrice, will you daddy?"

I shook my head. "No, baby," I said, "I won't. I love you, Partner, and your mommy. I always will. She's inside my heart and she'll always be there in a special place."

Lila gave me a big grin. The loose tooth in the back of her mouth was starting to show signs of falling out.

I started to flag down a cab but Lila said that she wanted to walk and Partner seemed eager to get in some exercise. So we walked to the Institute holding hands and telling jokes. Jokes about silly old men who are embarrassed by pretty young women and don't know how to act.

On the way to the Institute, we stopped and listened to a street singer. The song he sang was a sad song about the loss of his wife. I knew the song and it dated back to the Mexican Revolution when a plague of influenza had ravaged the country and hundreds of thousands of men, women, and children had died.

> Oh, God (the song went) why does the evil one
> take my family in the night?
> I am a righteous man and I have harmed no one.
> I do not think you are my benefactor anymore
> and I will not bow down to you again in prayer.

The song was a reaction to the Catholic influence of the Conquistadors and the violent response of the revolution to the Church causing Mexico to break its ties with the Vatican. It was also about the loss of faith we all suffer when our loved ones pass on unexpectedly. Surely, I knew how such a thing could happen. It had happened to me when Jennifer died.

We stood and listened for awhile, but I started to get choked up and Lila got upset. We walked on to school, the wonderful mood we'd been in suddenly broken by the memory of death, a memory that would not leave us but stayed on as a reminder of the suddenness of change and how our lives are so often controlled by chance.

CHAPTER 9

That afternoon, we went to the shops near the Zocolo, the shaded square block with a band stand in the middle that defined the center of life in Mexican cities. We were to meet Patrice who had offered to help me buy Lila some dressy clothes for the party. Patrice had discreetly asked if we had formal clothes. How formal, I'd asked?

"In Mexico, when we have an important party and invite honored guests from Mexico City," she said, "very formal."

"Tuxedos?" I asked, thinking that she would laugh.

"Possibly," she replied. "But most of the men will wear a dark suit and dark tie."

I shook my head. "Patrice," I said, "I don't even have a suit in California, let alone here."

She wrote down the name of a shop near the Zocolo and suggested a time to meet. "I can meet you and help out," she said, but I wasn't very happy. A party with a suit was too much like a wedding.... or a funeral. Both events had awful associations in my mind.

Lila, Partner, and I walked from our condo off Morelos Sur and up the boulevard with the vendors on every street corner. We always tried to buy something from a different vendor even if we didn't need the things we bought. People were so poor that you tried to maintain their dignity by purchasing something.

Today we bought a braided belt for me for 21 new pesos. I tried it on and liked it immediately, but Lila just shook her head.

"What's wrong?" I asked.

"The color, daddy, it's not so nice."

The curse of my family. I was a little color-blind and too vein to admit it. Maybe she was right, but it looked good to me and we bought it anyway. I told her that I could wear it around the house and when I worked outside. It would be my Hemingway belt and I'd get a special buckle with the words, "Cowboy Professor" on it, but she just shook her little head at me as we walked toward the Zocolo.

We took a short cut through the Cathedral grounds and watched a marriage procession. When the pretty bride came out, the mariachis began to play. It was difficult to catch the words because everyone was singing along, even the little children in their finest clothes. Everyone looked happy and there was laughter and joking. The men wore the elaborate tuxedos they wear in Mexico and the women were dressed in the frilly lace dresses I had seen at the weddings of my Latino students.

How unlike the American weddings I had gone to where everyone looked uncomfortable and the unspoken animosities of the respective families hung in the air so that you felt the partnership was doomed before it even began.

In time, the Bishop came out and blessed everyone. I hoped the blessing included us and silently wished them good luck. They'd need it, I thought, and then scolded myself for being so cynical.

We meandered on toward the Zocolo past the shops and small cafes and the people who walked by us in no perceivable pattern. The city was alive after siesta and everyone looked very purposeful.

Patrice met us at a men's shop near the Zocolo. She greeted me with a kiss on the cheek. I could smell her perfume on my clothes all through the evening and it was a smell of lotus blossoms and exotic tropical plants that I could not identify.

"Hello, Sam," she said, but her voice was sweet and full of promise and I could not imagine a more beautiful sound anywhere in God's universe. She bent over and kissed Lila who looked uncomfortable and had that hangdog look children get when they think they are being abandoned.

Like tuxedos, they rented black suits. We had a difficult time finding the right size, however, both in length and, I hate to admit it, in width. I'd have to talk to Laticia tomorrow. Patrice saved the moment by observing that the men in Mexico were not quite as large as *Norte Americanos*. But I saw the owner of the store smile and knew what he was thinking. Too many Margaritas for the large Jewish professor from North America.

Then we walked to a shop nearby where everyone greeted Patrice warmly and the shop owner kissed her on both cheeks and inquired about her family. They brought out cold drinks and after chatting for awhile, we finally bought Lila a formal white dress and black pumps. She fidgeted and grumbled about the shoes being too tight, but she looked marvelous, like an angel, and I told her so. The news did not seem to brighten her day.

When we'd finished our shopping, Patrice asked if she could buy us an ice cream cone or an espresso and we walked to the store across from the Zocolo with 100 different flavors of ice cream and sat slowly eating our cones and watching the people go by, as is the custom in Mexico.

Patrice looked beautiful in the late afternoon sun. The stores in Cuernavaca close in mid-day for siesta and afternoon *comida,* and so we did not meet until almost sunset.

As we spoke of the many things that seemed so easily to come up in our conversations, I noticed how intently she seemed to listen to anything we said and, like some writers I've known, record the words in her mind for future reference.

"Do you write, Patrice?" I asked her.

"Why do you ask?" she said, cocking her head, an effect that made me shiver again.

"Because of the way you listen so carefully," I said. "It's like writers I have known."

"Yes, I write, but I am still not good at it, not like you, Sam," she said.

"You know my writing?"

"Oh, yes," she said. "I have read your book, *Remembering Zion,* about Jennifer. It touched my soul."

I shook my head in amazement. The book I'd written about Jennifer had only a very modest success in America. Perhaps Jean had given it to her and I asked.

"No," she said. "I knew of the book when it came out. I didn't know that it was a true story, however. We tend not to be so honest in our writing here in Mexico. It is a magical book, Sam. I was very moved. I wish one day to write so honestly."

She looked straight at me without a hint of caprice or guile.

"Perhaps I can read something you've written," I said, noticing the way her breasts heaved when she spoke. The effect was so forceful and dramatic that it made my head go absolutely blank. I felt my face get red and hot.

She shook her head. "No, Sam. It would…." and then she was at a loss for words. She thought for a moment and said, "It would embarrass me."

I sat looking at her trying to get myself together. I had not looked at a woman this way, truthfully, in seven years. That was a long tome in anyone's life to be so out of touch. I silently shook the cobwebs out of my mind and tried to respond to what she'd just said.

"A writer should never be so caught up in their egos as to be embarrassed, Patrice," I said. "You write so that others can read and learn. Let the reader be the judge. All the writer can do is to try their best and be honest and truthful to the story they are telling."

Boy, put out a book and you're the resident expert on everything. I looked over at Patrice. The amused look was gone. The look that came over her beautiful face after that moment was breathtaking. I could hardly breathe and I became dizzy.

"Ah, Sam," she said,. "You will break my heart and I will be unable to stop you."

I was dumb founded and looked at her to see if she was joking. But she wasn't. You did not, in this formal country, say something so intimate unless you meant it.

She held onto my hand. I wanted to sit with her holding her hand until hell froze over or until someone came along and said, "Hey, Sam, yoo-hoo, Sam, it's a dream. No woman this beautiful is going to sit and hold your hand. It will not happen in this lifetime."

But no one came to break our reverie and we sat in the silence of the moment, holding each other's hand and feeling the beat of our respective hearts.

I wanted to say something meaningful and poetic but I said this to her in Spanish: "I think, Patrice, that my heart is beating hard." My Spanish was not good enough to say what I was saying, but I went on anyway. "My heart has been broken by one beautiful woman. It would not mend if it were to be broken by another. I don't think I could allow anything to happen between us, Patrice, although my heart and my head are at war. I think I would not handle another relationship well and I must think of Lila who is without her mother and would find it confusing at this point in her life."

And she said, a look of absolute serenity and gentleness on her face, "I will not break your heart, Sam, but mend it and make it stronger than ever." Her Spanish was so beautiful that the words were like songs from her lips.

The mariachis walked over and sang us a beautiful love song as we sat near the Zocolo holding hands and feeling the moment of joy that comes over you when you've met someone you think you will care about and who will care about you. In this life, after adolescents, it doesn't happen so often that you can squander the experience. So we sat and looked happily at one another and let the mariachis play their lovely music and ate our ice cream and watched the people of the city walk by. I had not had such a happy moment in many years and I savored every second.

Lila looked at us and I saw her eyes mist over. I touched her face but she moved away. Patrice saw what had happened and nodded. She understood, I think, and it was one of those defining moments where what you say is underscored by someone's behavior.

"I must go, Sam. They need help for the party and I promised to be there. I will see you on Saturday?" she asked, but she didn't ask about whether I was coming but would I be there with her, and I nodded my head and looked my most serious and replied in formal Spanish, "I will be there on Saturday, and should you wish to dance with me, I would be honored. One cannot waste a new suit and tie, so I will look particularly good and I will be yours for the evening, and should you wish to see me again as friends, then we will see one another as often as you wish."

A helpless look came over her face, the kind of look that said, "I am utterly incapable of doing anything to stop this from happening and please don't hurt me." I knew the look very well. It was the look on my face the year I was with Jennifer when my heart was broken.

She stood finally and bent over and kissed Lila on the cheek and then me. I could taste her tears when we kissed. They tasted of Jasmine.

And then she was gone, blending into the crowded Zocolo with the people milling about, waiting for something wonderful to happen in their lives.

Lila looked at me, a dazed expression on her face. We did not talk about it but sat and watched the people walk by and the vendors try and sell us everything imaginable.

What they could not sell us was an explanation of what had just happened or instructions on how to handle the feelings that hung in the air like a warm mist after the rain.

After awhile, we walked across the street to the Zocolo and watched the mimes and puppeteers perform. I bought some homemade potato chips a vendor sold on the Zocolo that smelled of lime and salt, and we found a metal bench to sit on and sat for a very long time, immersed in the atmosphere of the Zocolo with the many people who walked by and the vendors and the sounds and smells of this most beautiful of places.

We sat for a long time watching the people. It seemed to me that all of Cuernavaca was out tonight, and that everyone had that special look in their eyes that said life was exciting and wonderful beyond description. Everyone had that look but the poor people who looked on like uninvited guests too broken to ever believe they could be so happy.

Finally, Partner got restless and I broke my rule about taking a cab. I was, in truth, too drained to walk home.

We had a small snack before Lila took her bath and prepared for bed. She looked small and alone and would not speak to me. She turned her little face from me whenever I asked her anything until I finally gave up and suggested that she take her bath.

Before I tucked her in for bed, I overheard her prayers.

"Dear God," she said, "please don't tell my mommy about that lady, Patrice. Mommy's happy in heaven and she wouldn't like to know. My daddy is a nice man. Please help him choose a nice woman. Somebody," she seemed to add as an after thought, "who won't break his heart."

I went back to the living room and tried to read, but my mind was in turmoil and I couldn't concentrate. Why was it that when you were trying to find happiness, you always ended up hurting someone else? I looked at my reflection in the window and shook my head. There was something to say for being emotionally numb and I tried to will myself back to that familiar state, but couldn't.

As I sat on the sofa lost in my thoughts, the phone rang. There was no one on the line. It happens in Mexico a great deal because the phone system is still primitive, but I knew that it was Jennifer and my heart began to beat like mad.

I stood there holding the phone to my ears saying her name again and again, but no one answered and I felt the same anxiety come over me when calls from her would wake me in the night and her fear of death would hang over the dark like a tomb.

I put the phone down. My hands were shaking and I walked out on the back deck and sat in the dark. I could hear the night sounds and the music from a far away party. The frogs from the river were croaking and the Cicadas made a peculiarly Mexican noise as they sang out their love songs. In the background I could hear a voice and thought that it was coming from the street. It was a voice like a wounded animal. The closer I listened, the more distinct it became until I could make out every word.

The voice kept crying out, "Juan, oh, Juan, how can you be so cruel to me?" It was said again and again until I had to walk inside and close the door to the deck. I didn't want to hear the voice anymore. It was like the voice of someone drowning, or the pleading of someone who was about to be executed. It was the voice of my friend, Jean Henry, and I felt like a voyeur who intrudes on the violation of a soul.

That night I dreamt of rafting down the Colorado when Jennifer told me that she couldn't see me again and I awoke in a night sweat and couldn't return to sleep. I walked to Lila's room to look in on her, past the picture of the angel bringing her mother back to earth, and felt a pain in my heart that lingered for a long while. It was the pain of not wanting to hurt my daughter and the fear that we would both get hurt, anyway.

Lila slept soundly, her face like a sculpture of a tiny Madonna. I wanted to hold her tight and to tell her that I loved her very much, but I let her sleep and hugged Partner instead. He licked my hand.

CHAPTER 10

When you live in Mexico, you become accustomed to the noises and sounds of the city, for Mexico is a place of music playing, and car horns beeping,and people speaking to one another. It is a place of life and you feel the pulse of the city by the sounds that are made.

This morning, the birds were chirping. I could hear a dog barking in the distance and the vendors on the street selling tamales, and the chewing gum vendor singing, "*Chick-laaays! Por favor, amigos, Chick-laaaays!*"

The sun was shining through the window leading out to the deck and I rolled over in my bed feeling very lazy. I could hear Lila watching Mexican television in her room and talking to Partner. It was, I realized, time to get up and start the day.

I rolled out of bed and went into Lila's room and took a vote as to what we should do about breakfast. How about La India Bonita, I suggested. I had a strong hankering for a cup of their marvelous coffee.

"Will that Patrice be there?" Lila asked, not, I must add, in the kindest of voices I'd ever heard from the child.

"Uh-uh, just us and a delicious cup of hot chocolate and maybe some sticky roles. It's Friday, and the sticky roles are the best on Friday."

I took a vote. Two for La India Bonita and one abstention from Partner. He wanted to stay home and watch the cartoons on Mexican television, so we let him. Lila told me later that there was a cartoon about a dog and he hated to miss it because it was sort of like a soap opera.

The waitresses at the restaurant were particularly catty today making references to how the Señor was dating women much too young and beautiful for someone his age, and that he would have his heart broken. But what, they said, could they do about it other than to serve coffee and try to be decent waitresses? They weren't smart *Norte Americanos*, but just lowly waitresses.

Did my Jewish mother follow me everywhere I went, I wondered?

Lila was in a much better mood this morning. She'd discussed my relationship with her mother last night, she informed me. Her mom seemed to think that Patrice was an O.K. enough person although, in her opinion, she was a little too young for me. Anyway, if it was all right with her mom, it was alright with her, Lila told me.

I felt so grateful, you have no idea.

Were children always such killjoys? Had my first daughter Rachel been like this? Who could remember? I was so into academia then that all I could remember was waking up at five in the morning to write and only vaguely remembered Rachel getting up and putting on her snow suit and her mother, Alex, taking her off to kindergarten in the dead of winter, before it was even light out.

Like so many men in the early stages of their careers, I squandered my parenthood because of the need to prove myself in a world in which you can never prove yourself. It is a world so cloistered, and rigid, and self-absorbed with its own importance that it destroys and discards people, good people, people who have worked hard and care but don't have the stomach for the politics and the unending attacks on their competence.

I thanked Lila for allowing me to see Patrice, although the sarcasm probably went right by her. Did her mother have anything else to say, I wondered?

Lila shook her head. "Nope," she said, attacking her breakfast like there was no tomorrow.

Just then, at the oddest time, I looked up at the door leading to the street outside of the restaurant and saw Jennifer walk by. It took my breath away and I sat watching Lila eat her breakfast, my heart beating so fast I thought I would pass out.

I excused myself and walked outside to look for her but, of course, she wasn't there. She was in my heart and my heart played tricks on me at the oddest moments.

When I returned to our table, Lila looked up and smiled. "Did you see mommy, too?" she asked.

I nodded my head and watched the grin spread over her little face in triumph.

I sat for a long time feeling numb inside. Watching Lila eat her breakfast, I remembered a time in Zion when her mother had taken me to Flanagan's for eggs benedict. We sat in the restaurant and watched the sun send its light through the stained glass windows making lovely shapes and pictures on the walls. Jennifer looked at me that morning before the illness had taken over and held my hand.

"Oh God, Sam," she said, her lovely eyes so alive and clear in the morning light," I do love you so. Sometimes it makes my heart ache when I think about you."

My heart ached now for her and I sat at the breakfast table with Lila and felt morose and empty. Then I realized that the waitresses were starring at me and I shook off my daydreams and drank my coffee, although it felt like lead in my stomach.

Later in the morning, in my class, we talked about the Latino notion of love and I read some love poems and translated each of them into English, worried that I'd missed a nuance or a word and that the poems would lose their meaning. The one I liked best was by Gabriel Ramirez, a poet of the revolution that went:

The flowers of Vallarta are deep and red
and I am weary from this ride to fight
for Mexico.
My heart aches when I think of you,
my true love
and I remember your soft skin
when we made love
and our promise to be with one another
in God's arms,
after the struggle.

I will not leave you, my love
or let your memory flicker in my soul.
You are the companion of my heart
and I love you, my blessed one,
as if you were here with me
on this perfect beach,
the Pacific our bedroom and protector,
our shelter from the night.

As I read the poem, I looked downstairs at several people having coffee in the patio area and saw Patrice Gutierez listening to me read. I couldn't see her well enough to know what her eyes or face were saying, or whether she knew that the poem made me think of touching her face and the jolt that went through me when my hand felt her skin and warm tears ran slowly across my fingers.

There is a saying that a man who truly loves one woman is blessed, but that a man who loves two women at the same time, is cursed. I don't know which of those states I was in. There was no denying the visceral impact that Patrice Gutierez had on me. And yet, whenever I thought about the feelings that run rampant when one cares deeply about a woman, I thought of Jennifer and a glow of warmth would come over me.

Patrice walked over to me as I sat alone after class waiting for Lila to finish her Spanish lessons. She kissed me lightly on the cheek, the smell of perfume on her soft skin so exotic and tantalizing that it made me dizzy.

She sat down across from me on the old metal chairs they used at the Institute and told me that she had overheard me reading the poetry of some of her favorite writers.

"How did you know Ramirez?" she asked. "He is certainly an obscure poet, even by Mexican standards."

She wore a simple print dress and sandals with a single strand of pearls. She looked even more beautiful than the last time I had seen her, if that was possible.

She touched my hand. I could feel her pulse. My heart was thumping out a message in some primeval code. I didn't know what to say or what to do. Then I got my courage back and looked at her and told her the truth.

"I found all of the poems on love," I said, finally, "that I would have wanted to read to you personally, and this was the one I liked the most."

She looked at me, her mouth opened slightly, a quizzical look on her face. "Perhaps I can return the favor," she said, and opened a notebook and read slowly in Spanish. This is what she said as I translated the poem into English.

> Mi Corazon (my heart) is a brimming bottle.
> Open it and out will pour a lifetime of love.
> I have saved it for a special one
> who does not know or understand
> how his presence touches me.
>
> He will not fade away in my mind
> only to form a forgotten memory,

For he is tender as the dove
and resolute as the eagle in flight.

In Spanish, the words hummed along like a song a bird would sing in the early morning rain.

When Patrice read the poem, her voice was so gentle and soft that I was transported to another place and time. It was when I met Jennifer, and she told me that she loved me, and the world stopped being itself and became a place of magic.

"I wrote it for you, Sam. It is my gift to you," she whispered.

The birds sang in the trees when Patrice said that, and the wind died down to a whisper, and the world stood still.

I held Patrice's hand in mine and could only wonder at how strange, indeed, were God's workings.

Later, Lila and I walked home after her class. She chattered away about class and how well she had done, not having mastered the self-deprecation that we adults use to diminish our talents so that we don't seem immodest.

I looked at her and a feeling of intense love came over me. I can't explain why in that moment it happened, but I took her small hand and we walked together, and I breathed in her voice and marveled at the wonders of her mind.

Lila looked up at me and held my hand in that moment. My face felt flushed and I knew that we needed to get home as quickly as we could.

As we walked home, I said a prayer to God for Lila because I couldn't risk the thought that something might happen to her. It was the prayer I'd said for my daughter Rachel when she was only two and had begun to read and could spell already. It went:

How sweet are the gifts of the mind, oh, Lord.
Pray that we will be content and that arrogance
will not diminish us in your eyes.

CHAPTER 11

The day was coming to a close and twilight came with its peaceful and serene calm. I sat alone outside on the back deck and watched the Cuernavaca sun change the colors of the sky a hundred or more times.

Patrice was on my mind. I could smell her perfume on my clothing and suddenly felt a sense of contentment I hadn't felt in a very long time.

I was attracted to Patrice in a way I could not understand or control. Perhaps it was *Beshert*, as we say in Yiddish. Perhaps it was our destiny. Could you experience *Beshert* with two people? I was doubtful but I knew that I had certainly experienced it with Jennifer and I vowed to maintain a certain distance from Patrice, who came from a different culture and had all the trapping of someone who would break my heart with a kiss.

The birds were singing love songs. I wanted to join them but wondered who the love song belonged to, Patrice or Jennifer? It made me uncomfortable to think about.

But then Lila came out on to the deck and ended my reverie. "Daddy," she said, "there's a man outside who wants to talk to you."

I got up from the chair and walked to the front door. To my surprise, it was Manuel Gutierez, Co-Director of the Institute and Patrice's brother.

We traded greetings and I asked him to join me on the deck for a drink. We walked outside and sat and watched the beautiful sunset together in silence. We didn't know one another well enough for small talk and the silence of the moment proved to be enough of an icebreaker to resolve our initial discomfort.

Finally, he put his drink down and turned to me.

"I was in the neighborhood, Sam," he said, "and I thought that I would stop by and see how you were."

"Fine, Manuel, we're all just fine. The house is lovely and everything goes well for us," I said.

"Good. I'm glad, Sam. Jean was right to ask you to come. You have added a special something to the Institute and we appreciate it," he said.

I thanked him and we sat looking at the sunset together, neither of us uncomfortable or anxious enough to say anything else.

"Sam, I am not to talk to you about Patrice. It would hurt her very much if she knew that we were talking about her. She has warned me to stay away from you, but I am her older brother and the head of the family since my father died, and I cannot."

My heart was pounding. I knew something awful was about to be said.

Manuel looked at the sunset and watched a plane fly very high overhead on its way to somewhere exotic like Peru or Brazil. He turned from the plane and looked at me again in that distracted way Mexican men have of speaking to foreigners. He didn't quite look at me but looked through me.

"Look, Sam. We are a very old family in Mexico. I must say it because there is no way to avoid the subject. It would not be right for you and Patrice to be involved. She is," he said, looking at two birds mating as they hopped up and down on a limb of a branch, "spoken for."

Spoken for. What an interesting concept. I wondered who had done the speaking?

I looked at Manuel and smiled, I think, a warm and agreeable smile. I didn't strike out or speak harshly as anyone would expect a silly gringo like me to do, especially one who had begun to like someone very much who was..... well, spoken for. I just sat and watched Manuel shuffle about in his chair, a flush coming over his face as he became more and more uncomfortable.

"Sam," he continued, "you can see that it would be best if you told Patrice that the two of you must not become involved. It would look very bad for the family and it would exact a toll on Patrice. We are a people who are set in our ways. You may not agree with the way we do things in Mexico, but you must respect them as our way, just as I learned to respect your ways when I married an American woman."

I ran my hand over the frost from the glass and looked at the sun through the bottom. It looked distorted and surreal.

Manuel sat in his chair, squirming, waiting for me to capitulate for, as he so quaintly put it, the good of the family and, of course, the traditions of the country. I let him squirm.

Finally, I looked over at him, the agreeable look still on my face and I said:

"I believe, Manuel, that in Mexico such business is not done in a man's home. So you have dishonored me by coming here rather than choosing a neutral place."

Manuel made a motion to let me know that I was misunderstanding him, but I shrugged it off.

"Then you further dishonor me by trying to enter my private life. Our relationship does not permit you do that. Not now or ever again."

Manuel fell back in his chair, a look of resignation on his face.

"Finally, it is Patrice who decides whether I will interfere with a family arrangement. Do not ask me to stop something we may both wish to happen because it makes your life easier. I cannot countenance such interference in my personal life, and I will not permit you to speak of it any further."

I looked him in the eyes and still had that agreeable and reasonable look on my face that I had developed as a professor when students said things so inane or thoughtless that you wanted to run from the room screaming and give up teaching.

"I will not tell Patrice of our meeting or what transpired here," I continued. "I will not agree to stop seeing her. That is something she will have to decide. And finally, I will not attend your party or dishonor myself by being in your presence."

I said all of this in very precise Spanish and as formally as I could so that it would have the most meaning to him. Then I turned from him and set my sights on the setting sun and the colors of the sky as they danced across the horizon.

But I saw his face as he was leaving. It was red and flushed, and a small vein above his right eye pulsated as if it would burst.

I sat in the chair for a long time and watched the sky darken. In the distance, the ever-present music came and went like waves on the beach. A dog barked and the crickets chirped as night began to fall.

I didn't speak to Patrice of the conversation with her brother. It never came up again but, as with all things in Mexico, it hung over us in the background and made the noises of the wind before the storm.

Jean, however, spoke to me later in the evening. She looked drained of life. I fixed her a drink and we sat on the deck after Lila had fallen asleep. Partner sat next to me, his paw on my foot.

"Sam," she said, "I don't interfere in the business of friends, but I will say just one thing. If you involve yourself with Patrice, it won't work out. It can't. This is Mexico and family means everything here. If you offend family then you have no ballast to keep yourself afloat. Patrice will have pressures put on her that you just can't imagine. It will destroy her and it will destroy you. Don't let yourself get hurt again, Sam."

I wanted to tell her about the conversation I'd heard the other night in which she sounded like a wounded animal and to ask her what gave her the idea that she could talk to me that way, but I didn't. We were old friends and sometimes you let old friends say things that you ordinarily wouldn't let anyone else say.

We sat in silence and let the night bugs fly around us as if they were clearing the air between us.

"One other thing, Sam," she said. "I need you to come to the party, as a favor to a friend. These are hard times in Mexico. I don't know that we can stay afloat much longer without help. The people at the party can help us, Sam. They'll be impressed that you're part of Las Hispañas. Everything here is done in backrooms, as favors given or favors returned. This is a favor, a very large one. Put your animosities toward Manuel behind you and be nice to everyone. For one night, old friend, please do me this favor."

I sat and thought of the doctor who had been so nasty to me when Jennifer had her surgery and how I wished that I had been particularly nasty in return. The small hurts became big hurts in time if you didn't deal with them, but Jean was a friend and I agreed to come to the party. You came through when friends needed you, otherwise you had no business calling yourself a friend.

"O.K., I'll come," I said, "but only on one condition."

"Yeah? And what's that," she said suspiciously.

"That you tell me why you never went out with me when we were in graduate school. It really fries me all these years later, you know that, Jean?"

"Ah, boychick, now that is, as they say in the English Navy, a story that needs the hair of the dog to be told correctly. Get me another drink, keep the tequila coming, and I'll tell you a story about old Jean and why some young punk from North Dakota who asked her out then would not have had a chance in hell."

And she did. And like old times, we sat on the deck getting drunk on tequila and laughing so hard La Señora's light came on several times. It was good to hear her laugh and to know that I had a true friend in Mexico.

But when she left, a sadness came over me and I couldn't help but think that anyone close to me was doomed. I vowed to not let myself get so close to Patrice that we would hurt one another. And then I resolved to be strong and mighty as the river and a warrior in matters of the heart.

We wait for the light, and instead, there is
darkness.
We look for meaning in life, but we are without sight.
We wait for justice, but there is none.
We speak lying words and utter them
from the heart.
For our transgressions against you are many
and our sins are testimony
against us.

CHAPTER 12

About the party, I have little to say. Patrice looked her most beautiful in a long formal gown that made her look even more like a movie star or a model, she was that lovely.

I did the work for the Institute to help them because I believed in their work and I wanted to help. I even wore the suit we had rented, although I felt like an old fool in my black tie and formal shirt. It made me think of the joke we used to tell in high school about how one of my friends walked up to a mortician in our hometown and asked him how business was. "Dead," said the mortician, "absolutely dead."

That's how I felt in a suit and black tie.

Lila looked lovely and within minutes, a group of children had surrounded her and taken her off to another part of the house to play games. Her Spanish was improving so quickly that she could converse with them with no difficulty.

Manuel Gutierez and I avoided one another. His lovely wife Harriet, an American anthropologist whom he had met at Berkeley, took me aside to apologize for Manuel's bad handling of our conversation.

"This is not 1895," she said, "when such things were done, and Manuel knows it. Patrice is a grown woman and she can do as she pleases, Sam. Don't be mad at Manuel. He isn't very good at these sorts of things. You and Patrice are adults. You'll work things out as adults do, I'm sure."

I nodded my head and politely thanked Harriet but inside, where I lived, in my heart of hearts, I could never forgive such conduct.

It was very Jewish of me, I'm afraid, for we believe in retribution. It was us who said, after all, "An eye for an eye and a tooth for tooth."

The party was really a huge public relations ploy, but the women were beautiful and well dressed, and the Mexico City politicos were unctuous and suave and clearly the reason for the horrible shape Mexico was in.

They were all American educated. Harvard, MIT, Berkeley, Yale. I shuddered to think what that meant for the health of our nation's great institutions of learning.

One of the politicos who engaged me in conversation, Manuel Ortiz, a Wharton School of Management Ph.D., later absconded with over one hundred million dollars of oil money from the national treasury.

In Mexico they called the national treasury a savings account for the politicians who daily made their illicit withdrawals at will.

Whenever North Americans get angry about the corruption in Mexico, however, it's important to remember that the corruption began with the Aztecs, who extorted and plundered their neighbors, grew to a fevered pitch with the bloody Spaniards, and continued on, as a national pastime, with the thieving politicians before, during, and after the Mexican Revolution.

Countries do not always develop in the mystical way America did, but have national flaws so glaring that they never fully recover. When you have official corruption for 1,000 years or more, it becomes a difficult thing to stop.

I looked over at Patrice, who was talking gaily to a guest and his wife in that beautiful voice of hers and in Spanish so lovely that the words seemed to dance from her lips.

Two men were playing guitar and singing the old Mexican love songs that even North Americans know. I listened to them sing the melancholy love songs and thought how bitter sweet love could be and how it is more wonderful and more awful then anyone who has never been in love can ever imagine.

Patrice walked over to me, her honey blond hair long and straight to the middle of her back. She came up to me and kissed me on the cheek, and said in that low voice of hers, "Hello Sam, I have missed you."

I was no longer embarrassed or shy in her presence and took her hand and kissed it, something I had never done before. It just seemed the right thing to do.

"You are so beautiful tonight that angels bow to your beauty and fly to heaven to tell the gods the news." I said this in Spanish which made such a statement sound even more beautiful than it was.

And she replied, "And you, my love, are like the stars in the heavens announcing the arrival of love."

We stood looking at one another, holding hands, swaying to the music until gradually, effortlessly, we held one another and began to dance. I could feel her breasts against my chest.

It felt timeless to be in Patrice's arms. Timeless and as gentle as the first leaf on a tree in spring or a flower in bloom with dew on it's peddles. I drew in a breath and held Patrice in my arms. It was like gliding on air or flying through the sky on the wings of a dove. I felt lost within her presence, and I could not hear the people around us or the music playing somewhere very far away. All I knew was that we were alone in space and time in our own private galaxy.

The sensation of timelessness seemed to go on forever and I was so moved that I couldn't think that this was happening to me. She whispered something in my ear and, at first, I couldn't hear what she said because I was still in her arms and far away in another place. And then she said it again and I heard her words and a small jolt went through me.

"I love you, *mi amor*," she said, "I love you my beautiful Sam. I cannot help myself. I do not wish to love anyone, but I *do* so love you and I cannot help myself."

When she said this to me, a light flashed in my head and everything turned white for a second. We held each other and danced into the night, lost in our private world.

Patrice held me in her arms and we danced to a slow and mournful Mexican ballad whose words said, "Silent are the tears that fall from a heart that is broken."

We danced on in the beautiful Cuernavaca night and all that I could think about was the poetry that ran through my mind. I remembered another of the poems of Ramirez that I'd read to my class and whispered it to Patrice as we danced in our little corner, our special place in the world.

> The guns of war frighten me.
> I stand in fear of death.
> But in my love for you I am fearless
> and I will kiss you in my heart
> to make the fear leave,
> on the wings of angels.

Later in the evening when people began to leave the party for the long drive back to Mexico City, Patrice walked us to the car. She held my hand, kissed me on the cheek and on the lips, and then she held me tight. Lila looked on but the happy smile on her face did not leave. She had resigned herself, I think, that her mad old Jewish dad was acting weird and that it was alright, even though she doubted he knew what he was doing.

"Until tomorrow, my love," Patrice whispered in my ear.

As we drove home, Lila said, "She's so pretty, dad, she looks like a movie star."

I nodded and wondered what was happening to me. I was a child of the Holocaust. Like all of us raised in the aftermath of that singularly heinous event, I was raised not to trust anything that might be unlikely to happen in the ordinary day to day activities of life.

In my world, beautiful women did not meet or fall in love with ordinary men like me. I couldn't reconcile the truth of my upbringing with the reality of my experiences. It had happened twice now in my life when it should not have happened at all.

We drove through the Cuernavaca night and a summer storm began to blow the rain in angular lines against the car window. Lila had fallen asleep, her little body resting against mine. I looked over at her and a rush of love enveloped me. I didn't distrust my love for Lila or fear my luck with her. She was my link to Jennifer, my link to life.

We drove on through the summer night, the rain beating down hard now against our car. I should have pulled over and let it pass but I knew that God protected us that night and would not let anything happen. The summer storm outside and the turmoil inside made me think of a poem by Mark Strand called *The Remains*, which said exactly what I wished I could do.

> I empty myself of the names of others. I empty my pockets.
>
> I empty my shoes and leave them beside the road.
>
> At night I turn back the clocks;

CHAPTER 13

In the next few weeks, Patrice and I tried to make the most of our time together. I would be in Cuernavaca until early August and then we would need to return to my job and Lila's start of first grade. We decided to see as much of Mexico as we possibly could with Patrice as our tour guide.

We went to Acapulco the weekend after the party with Lila and Partner. Patrice drove the new toll road to the ocean, the world's most expensive toll road where a 120 mile trip cost the equivalent of $150.00, American. Patrice didn't have the same feeling for "Chevy Joe" as the rest of the family, and we ended up in a BMW the size of North Dakota.

We stayed at the Princess Hotel, a luxury resort near the high rocks where divers time their dives with the waves as they crash against the rocks to please the rich tourists. I could not count myself in the category of rich tourist, but we did see the divers and it was exhilarating and frightening to watch. Life was cheap in Mexico and every year any number of poor children hurt or killed themselves practicing the dives they hoped would land them a job showing off to the wealthy patrons of the hotel.

It was surely the most luxurious place I'd ever stayed in. Given my salary as a professor, perhaps that wasn't saying a lot, but it was really fantastic. Each bungalow had a special view of the Pacific and the furnishings and the service were on the opposite end of the scale of Motel 6 and the other places we usually stayed. We stayed in separate rooms. I explained to Patrice that I wasn't ready for intimacy and that it was difficult for me to think that I ever would be ready. I said these things while my body was telling me the exact opposite. I suspect Patrice knew how I really felt and agreed to our arrangement, unhappily I think. Plus, there was Lila, and her feelings about her mom were such that any violation of my love for Jennifer would have been seen as a betrayal in her 5 year-old mind.

The desk clerk bowed slightly when we arrived and told us that he was honored to have one of the country's leading writers among their guests. I looked around to see if someone else was standing with us, but it was just the three of us. Partner didn't count.

I looked at Patrice, but she waved her hand and we were on our way to the beautiful bungalow which would house us for the next few days. On the way to the room, I saw an American actress sitting out by a private pool. It was all that I could do not to gawk and make a fool of myself. I was, after all, not so far from my roots in North Dakota that seeing a movie star failed to bring the hay seed out in me.

Later, Patrice and I sat on the beach as Lila and Partner cavorted in the ocean. I'd never seen Lila so tanned and healthy looking before. The waves came in and Lila would jump in them and laugh and scream as they knocked her over. Partner would run over to see if she was alright and then she'd get up and jump in the waves all over again. Finally, she got the timing down and could do it without getting knocked over.

We stayed out in the sun until late afternoon, washing ourselves off in the outdoor showers by the beach. I looked over at Lila before we went in. She was as happy as I had ever seen her. So was I, for that matter.

That night before dinner, we looked out of the window of our bungalow at the sun setting and if God wasn't hovering over us, I don't know where he was. Because the colors of the sky were so beautiful, so powerful and distinct, that only God in heaven could have been personally responsible.

We dressed for dinner. Patrice wore a long dress, as was the custom in Mexico, and a hat to keep her hair from blowing in the wind. Lila had on a simple white dress and sandals, and her hair was done in a French braid which made her look just like her mother.

People looked at us as we walked in and a hush fell over the restaurant as if royalty had arrived. I looked behind us again to see if some famous person was standing in line, but it was us they were looking at. For a second time that day, I had the feeling that I'd not been let in on all there was to know about Patrice Gutierez.

We were seated outdoors with a beautiful view of the Pacific. The wind cooled the air and it felt clean and comfortable after the day on the beach.

"You look wonderful," I said to Patrice who smiled and kissed my hand in response.

"I love you, Sam," she whispered and touched my cheek with her long delicate fingers.

I noticed a young woman look over at Patrice, hesitate, and finally screw up the courage to approach her.

She came over to the table and politely asked Patrice for an autograph. She said that she adored Patrice's work and was a great fan. Patrice obliged and thanked her for stopping by.

When the young lady left, I raised my hands in the universal sign that asked, "What gives?"

"It is nothing, Sam, nothing," she said, taking a sip from her drink.

She looked away and would not talk about it.

"Patrice," I said, "Talk to me. Why did she ask for your autograph?"

"It is nothing, Sam. I have done a few articles for magazines in Mexico. We are a small country, really. People know you easily."

But later I discovered that wasn't quite it. I was sitting in the lobby and someone had left *Liberacion*, the South American literary magazine. I was leafing through it and there, before my embarrassed eyes, was an article about Patrice. It called her the next very great Latina poetess. Several of her poems were printed. They were in Spanish but, whatever the language, they were very great poems.

The magazine went on to say that she was educated at Radcliff College and had published poems in America and Mexico. The magazine listed the awards that she had won, some of which were major awards that even I had heard of. She had a B.A. in literature from Radcliff and a M.F.A. from Sara Lawrence in creative writing. And then it gave an abbreviated bibliography, which made me want to hide my head in the vast amount of sand outside of our bungalow and look for some crow to eat.

What an idiot I'd been. Me, of all people, lecturing someone with Patrice's gifts about the honesty of writing.

I told her about the article and how silly I felt for lecturing her on the Zocolo about the honesty of writing and other things I knew next to nothing about. And you know what that beautiful woman said, that talented woman with more ability in her little finger than I had in my whole body? She said:

"Sam, I do not love a man for his talent, or for his money, or for his possessions. I love him for his soul. And yours, my love, is true, and brilliant, and tender. It is translucent to me, Sam. I can see inside of you. I cried on the Zocolo because I saw inside of your heart when you were speaking. I did," she said, and she would not talk about her writing anymore.

But she let me read her poetry, and, as God is my witness, it was the poetry of an angel. I felt a sense of sheer joy at seeing such talent. It made me feel small and insignificant in her presence. Luminous was the word for her poetry. It glowed.

After I read her poetry, my feelings were even more confused. A little Jewish monster hid inside my head and said, "Uh-uh, Sam, be careful now. She might hurt you if you let her. Hang back. Don't get too close. Didn't you get hurt enough with Jennifer?" Yes, yes I did get hurt, but it didn't stop me from looking at Patrice in a new way and wondering if this gentle person, this sensitive poet could hurt a fly.

We stayed that weekend in the beauty of Acapulco and treasured the tropical splendor and the warm ocean water that cured the ills of the world when you were in its clutch. We swam and Lila and I went on the yellow banana, the long rubber inner tube with stirrups towed by a speed boat where I did a header into the sand when the boat stopped and the yellow banana tipped over. Lila laughed so hard at me, with my head full of wet sand, that she keeled over into the water. Ah, children, count on them to be there when you are at your most clumsy.

Before we left, we had a wonderful meal on the boulevard which parallels the beach and has hundreds, it seemed to me, of great Mexican restaurants. We also took Lila to the Hard Rock Cafe and had American style hamburgers and listened to 60's rock music. Mexico was beating up on America in soccer and all of the Mexican help were cheering whenever a Mexican goal was made. There was a great deal of cheering that evening.

We bought Lila a Hard Rock Cafe tee-shirt, which she wore most of the following day until I suggested we wash it and after that, most of the rest of the following week. She still wears it although it is too small for her. Children outgrow everything, it seems to me, in their rush to be adults.

We said goodbye to Acapulco late Sunday afternoon. If there is a more beautiful place on earth in the late afternoon when the sun begins to set, and the lights come on, and the hotels along the ocean glisten at dusk, and the water sparkles as far off in the horizon as you can see, I don't know where it is.

On the ride back to Cuernavaca, Lila and Partner slept in the back seat and Patrice and I held hands and spoke little as we drove the beautiful, but strangely empty toll road that only the rich could afford to drive. We were serene and sleepy from our wonderful weekend, which I would never forget, and I felt lucky to be with Patrice and didn't want to break the spell by saying anything.

We drove into the night and listened to the beautiful love songs on the radio. Nowhere in the world is the poetry of love songs more beautiful than it is in Mexico. It was a dream time as the sun set and cast long shadows over the land before it became dark and we would be left in the night with our thoughts of love and other things too personal to discuss.

> Oh, my love, I do not wish to speak
> For it would ruin this perfect moment.
> I have such love for you
> but it must wait
> when words and thoughts are from the heart
> and the Gods of Love enchant our night
> and touch our world of dreams.

CHAPTER 14

During the week, after I had to taught and Lila was asleep with Jean watching her, the two of us would go to Las Mañanitas, the most beautiful restaurant in Cuernavaca, perhaps in all of Mexico, and watched the wild birds walk about the flowered grounds while we held hands and spoke about what had happened in our day.

Sometimes, we would dance in the bar and hold one another tight, not wanting to let go, even when the music stopped.

One evening we argued over nothing that I could understand and Patrice cried openly in the bar. If I could have slit my wrist in public, I would have. People looked at me as if I was a monster.

"Patrice," I said, "I'm so sorry. I apologize for whatever I did to upset you," even though I had no idea of what it was.

And she looked up at me and said, her beautiful eyes filled with tears, "I did not expect such meanness from you, Sam. You can be so cruel when you want to be. And you, a professor of psychology who does not know what he did to hurt someone he cares about."

"I do care about you, Patrice," I said, realizing that Patrice's sensibilities were light years beyond mine, vowing to be more careful in the throwaway lines I sometimes used, the clever little California sarcasms that protect us from people, even people we cared for.

Slowly, she would get over the hurt, look at me with eyes filled with tears and a look of betrayal on her face so strong that I would have committed myself to the Buddha, or gone to Tibet to ask the Dali Lama for forgiveness rather than to see her cry.

And when she was not hurt anymore, she would touch my knee or hold my hand and a jolt of pleasure would pass through me. Sometimes she would sing me songs of love that she had written. Songs of delicate beauty and sincerity that are in my heart forever.

One night she said to me, "Sam, you have ruined me for anyone else. I could not love anyone so much as I love you. Never."

What we argued about at Las Mañanitas that night was her intended, although in Spanish there is another word to define that status. And what I said was that it seemed absurd to make promises about marriage when two people didn't know one another.

No, that isn't what I said at all. Let me be honest. What I said to Patrice that evening, because of pride, and jealousy, and ego, and a hundred things that plague men and can make us jealous little monsters when we begin to care about a woman was, "Do you have a relationship with him, Patrice?"

What I really meant was whether she was sleeping with him. This from a mature man who had been around the track a few times. This from a man who knew Mexico. And this, from a man who had met a women so substantial that such a deeply offensive remark would have been certain to hurt her beyond description.

I'm ashamed of myself now, of course. I'm ashamed of myself as I was with Jennifer when she refused to see me anymore and I accused her of having another lover. It was a despicable thing to say and I wanted to take it back as soon as the words came from my lips, but pride would not let me stop and they were the words of my insecurity, my anguish as a man fighting love who deep within himself believed that he didn't deserve the woman he was with.

As Einstein said, to underscore my terrible behavior, "The difference between genius and stupidity is that genius has its limits."

She looked at me with tears in her eyes and said, "How could you be so mean, Sam, to ask that of me?"

And I said, the little California tyrant that I'd become, the little boy-child of the golden state, I said, "You know what the Italians say? A woman of substance has two lovers. One in public and one in private. She loves neither but gains an advantage over both because she is above getting hurt."

They should have come and locked me up for such garbage, such hurtful garbage.

Later, as we were getting ready to return home, me to my house with Lila in bed and Partner prowling the apartment waiting to devour any intruder, and Patrice to the family home, she said:

"You have concerns, Sam? then you must meet Juan and discuss them with him. It is the Mexican way."

I would have rather eaten glass, but I agreed to meet him or Patrice would have been very hurt, and I had done enough hurting this evening for a lifetime.

We met at the bar of the Cabrillo Lounge, an old writer's hangout from the days when American journalists came to Mexico to cover the Communist Party and to report on Leon Trotsky who had been given asylum in Mexico by President Cárdenas, the only truly populist president to reign in 250 years of Mexican sovereignty.

In those days, as today, Cuernavaca was the summer retreat of the rich and famous who wanted to escape the terrible summer weather in Mexico City, where it rains each day and air pollutants fall over the city as dirty rain.

It was an appropriate place to meet, the lounge as dark as the core of my heart. I stood by the door and tried to let my eyes adjust to the dark. A voice called out my name and I walked to a corner of the bar hearing the conspiratorial voices of the Mexican businessmen talking about the political mess in Mexico City.

The man I met was neither an ogre nor a saint. He was, like Patrice, caught up in the family custom of arranging marriages so that families could meld their wealth and come out more wealthy and, therefore, more powerful as a result.

His name was Juan Guzman. Like Patrice, he was American educated and of European decent. He was neither handsome nor unhandsome. He was a regular man. I wanted him to be hateful and disgusting so that I could be morally superior. He was neither.

We shook hands and sat for awhile, neither of us in a large rush to lose the advantage by opening the conversation. Finally, he cleared his throat and began.

"Señor," he said in a pleasant voice, "this is not easy nor I do not wish to make it more unpleasant for either of us. Patrice is in love with you. She told me so last night. I am happy for her and congratulate you. She has longed for a relationship with someone special. That is difficult in my country because men here are frightened off by someone of Patrice's exceptional talent and beauty."

He paused to take a sip of his drink, looked at the men sitting at the bar, nodding slightly toward several, and continued.

"Our families have made a decision for us. We were not consulted. Like Patrice, I have someone in my life whom I love. It is not Patrice. Our relationship has always been like brother and sister. And yet, in Mexico, family is everything. Without family, we are nothing. We lose our status and all of our connections. If we displease or go against family, we are considered dead just, I believe, as Orthodox Jews would read the *Kaddish,* the prayer for the dead if a child married out of the faith. Am I not correct?"

I nodded my head, beginning to feel sick inside.

"There is already much talk about you and Patrice. She is what you might call a celebrity in Mexico. She is the poet that Carlos Fuentes and others have designated as the great female poetess of the century.

"At her age, this is a sign of such brilliance and promise that she is as well known as any soccer star in Mexico and beyond. In Latin America, poetry is vastly popular. Patrice was one of four young poets to fill Sanchez Stadium in Mexico City. The stadium holds more than 100,000 people."

The waiter came and brought us new drinks before our old ones were finished. He was a very old waiter and had the look of someone who was cynical about life and would not care if he were fired since it would confirm his view of the world and justify his cynicism.

"If we do not marry, it will certainly not hurt Patrice as a poet since her fame is large and we Latinos love acts of rebellion that arise from issues of the heart."

He drank the rest of his drink and started the next one. I wondered if the cynical waiter knew more about Juan Guzman than I had first assumed. When he was done, he continued.

"Her family would be offended, however. And such an act would lead to an estrangement, perhaps a complete break. Mexico is in desperate shape. Without our families melding their resources, neither of us might make it."

There it was. I understood it all completely. My grandparents had been the result of arranged marriages in Russia, and they had hated one another with an intensity and a passion that I can remember to this day. I was their go-between and I came to know the act of marriage without love and its consequences, first hand.

We spoke some more, but it was all ground noise and small talk, words and sentences without meaning. My heart felt so heavy when we were done that all I wanted to do was rush home and hug Lila and Partner and call Patrice and tell her that we were all running away on the very next plane. But I knew that it was not so easy. The great boxer Joe Lewis had said it, and no one yet had come up with a greater truth. He said, "You can run, but you cannot hide."

CHAPTER 15

We did not speak again of Juan Guzman but continued our non-intimate romance in a sort of frenzy. I would be going back to California in another month and that reality had the impact of forcing us to pack so many experience into a short period of time.

And so we went to every famous and not so famous place that Patrice could think of in Mexico. One weekend we all went to Puerto Vallarta and lay like lazy tourists on the beach. Another weekend we went to the Silver Canyons, Mexico's Grand Canyon.

Through these weeks, there was one constant. Cuernavaca was always there, the City of Eternal Spring. If it had ever been more beautiful, I do not know. But then, with someone like Patrice in your life, everything was beautiful.

I remember one time that we all went to the old Catholic Cathedral for the Mariachi Mass. Lila wore the dress she'd worn to the party earlier and her black pumps. People looked at us as we walked in. It was a constant reminder to me of Patrice's position in Mexico that we could go nowhere without people recognizing her.

I remember that the walls of the Cathedral were being treated so that the original murals conceived by the Franciscan Monks were exposed, murals of racial superiority and mistreatment of the native Indians. They had been done by the native people and the arrogance of the Spaniards had not permitted them to realize that the native painters were leaving a history of their mistreatment in this palace for the worship of God.

During the service, people turned and stared at us, but Patrice was used to it and ignored it all. I couldn't. It was all so new to me.

One day Jean showed me a story in the Mexico City newspaper, *Las Noticias*, which literally meant, the news. Like most Mexican newspapers, the stories were more gossip and scandal than hard news because hard news was often controlled by the government.

There, in a prominent place in the paper, was a picture of Patrice with, what one could loosely translate from Spanish as her paramour. Me. The story said that Patrice's intended, Juan Guzman, had threatened to remove the private parts of one unnamed American professor if the affair did not end. An unnamed source close to Patrice's family said that the family was beside themselves with grief and that the Bishop of Cuernavaca was a frequent visitor to the home these days to offer his prayers and support.

And then they reprinted a poem Patrice had written about love two years earlier, but they made it sound as if the poem was current and was about us. The poem was a tragic indictment of love and the impossibility of love lasting. The story asked, "Will this affair of the heart of Mexico's leading lady of poetry be doomed?"

In California when someone writes something about you and you disagree, you write a defense which they publish or you take them to court and sue them. In Mexico, if the paper says it, most people think that it must be true. A rebuttal would only reinforce the truth of the story.

We did not speak of the story but I could imagine that it was as upsetting to Patrice's as it was to me.

What we did was to continue our high life style and trips. And, as the other poet in my life would have said, "Dad, it was real bueno."

During the week, aside from my late night dinners at Las Mañanitas with Patrice and sleep deprivation which should have affected me but did not, our lives had a pleasant rhythm. At least once a week in the afternoon, when *comida* was over and we were done with our respective activities, the three of us would walk to *Tres Cinema* (Cinema Three), across the street from an outdoor restaurant called, simply, Pizza Y Pasta, where Lila and I ate one night when we were hungry for American style pizza served by waiters who looked like they were in the Cleveland mob. You get hungry for the real thing sometimes when you are in a foreign country.

I had an arrangement with the gentle theater manager who allowed Partner in because I had helped him with an emotional problem which interfered with his love life. He had been unable to pay and we had agreed, as was the custom in Mexico, to a trade.

Partner loved the movies, but especially loved the excellent Mexican pop corn that you could buy for 3 new pesos before you went into the theater. They hadn't heard that coconut oil was bad for you nor were they concerned about fat content, and the popcorn tasted like the real stuff we had when we were kids.

All of the movies were American, but they were dubbed in Spanish with English sub-titles. When they were not dubbed but had Spanish sub-titles, the difference between what the English words were and what the sub-titles read could be hilarious. Funnier than the movies.

Lila didn't care what we watched. She liked everything. Partner, however, was partial to stories of love. He liked cartoons and we watched *Pocahontas* three times that summer. It was for Partner, Lila kept insisting.

We also went bar hopping from time to time. Lila liked Sanborns, an American style bar and restaurant with a lovely bar that faced La Boulevard de Benito Juarez. To get there we'd take a bus up Juarez and then, because it often rains in the evening in Cuernavaca in the summer, a cab home.

In the bars we would see young Mexican boys and girls dating. It was not a pretty sight. Away from their friends and all alone to fend for themselves, the dates looked miserable to the observer. There were long periods of silence and the psychologist in me wanted to walk over and mediate or help them out. But they only continued to chain smoke American cigarettes and look forlornly around hoping that a friend might drop by to save them further embarrassment.

What kind of people sit at a bar and do not speak in Mexico? People in love.

The waiters liked Lila and brought her diet cokes with little umbrellas floating about. Or they would bring *chicharizo*, pork rinds, the national junk food of Mexico, which Partner particularly loved. Lila would tell me about her day and how well her classes went. Her Spanish was good enough by now that she could take care of herself in most situations.

It was the birthday of one of her classmates later in the week and everyone was invited to a birthday party after class that Friday. Lila and her teacher were doing the planning. They would get together, a conspiratorial look on their faces, and talk in hushed tones as if this would be the party of the century. There was talk about the magician Houdini coming to perform until someone realized that he'd been dead for more than 60 years. Someone said that if he came back from the dead, it would elevate magic to a new level.

What they did was to hire an excellent mariachi band and to have the birthday girl sit in the outdoor room on third floor we used for parties, not realizing that they were about to have a surprise party for her. Then suddenly, we all materialized out of nowhere, singing happy songs I didn't know. We all gathered around with the mariachi band and sang, "*Feliz Cumplianaos*" or, happy birthday. The melody was universal.

Later, the mariachi band sang my favorite Spanish song, *Malagueña Se Le Rosa,* a song I'd heard on the CBC growing up in North Dakota, which made me want to see Latin America and which was probably responsible for us being in Mexico that summer.

When you grow up in such an isolated place, you only have your imagination, really, to take you through the long, cold winters and the endless bouts of disasters that plague the people of the prairies. I wanted to sing in mariachi bands like the great *Trio Los Paraguyos* which I would listen to on the CBC from Winnipeg. To me, there could be no place more romantic or wonderful than Latin America, a belief I hold in my heart to this day.

Patrice and I sat together and held hands while the young Spanish teachers from the Institute clucked and spoke behind our backs, telling stories, I am sure, so embellished that they would come out absurd beyond description.

That summer, Patrice wrote very intimate and personal poetry about our love. When she spoke the poems she had written, *Dios mio!* my God, what beauty. Poetry is for the voice, and when it is read, it had a much different meaning than when it was written.

One night, the nightingales singing in great form outside the window of a restaurant in Cuernavaca and music from a party somewhere far off in the distance floating though the air barely loud enough to distinguish the words, Patrice read this poem to me:

I am a bird of paradise and you are an eagle.
We meet together and are mismatched.
You overpower me and I can only sing my songs of love.
Somehow, my strong and gentle eagle, we fly together,
to heights that a bird of paradise should not reach.

I have taught you to sing in my voice
and you have taught me to soar to the heavens.
It is the very meaning of love
and I will sing for you a lovely song
and you will share the song with everyone.
We are in love,
a love that is the greatest wonder.

"Sam, my dear one," Patrice said," I have re-read your book about Jennifer and do not think that we can all three be together in heaven. You must ultimately choose one of us."

But I could not.

Far in the distance, thunder rolled across the Valley of the Gods, the mythical valley of the Aztecs where Mexican history began, and the summer rain brought the sweet Cuernavaca smells through the open window.

That is the way I will always remember my time with Patrice. Poetic, biblical, passionate. The thunder we had heard earlier boomed across the sky and the summer rain beat down like cannon shots. God had spoken and we would never be the same. Patrice looked at me with sad eyes and understood that I must choose Jennifer, and that fact, alone, aside from the many pressures on her and the differences in our lives, would make loving me impossible. The truth of it made me very sad and I looked forlornly at Patrice whose eyes were filled with of tears and who had a look of despair on her face.

Chapter 16

In the weeks to follow, pressure was placed on Patrice to stop our relationship, which would have broken a lesser person. I knew none of these things or I would have ended our relationship to save Patrice the grief that she suffered in silence.

An important prize that Patrice had been assured she would win was given to a lesser poet. Fuentes and others protested, but to no avail.

A left wing literary journal of no consequence came out with an article that said the sort of romantic poetry Patrice wrote was the same nonsense that had kept Mexico poor and unliberated for almost 300 years. It was poetry for rich people and for those who could afford the time and the luxury of love. Most Mexicans, the writer said, "Were too poor, too troubled, and too oppressed to get through the day with enough food to eat, let alone to love in the stylized and romantic way that Patrice presented love." He called her, "The Rich Bitch Poet from Cuernavaca by way of Radcliff, Sara Lawrence, and *True Romance Magazine.*"

If I would have known about the article when it came out, I would have beaten the insulting little pig into the ground. They had done the same sort of hatchet job on Yevtachenko and Pasternak in Russia, and on every other talented writer and artist who didn't conform to the notion that art was for, and about, the masses. As if the masses did not love.

And yet, nothing changed in our relationship. We traveled here and there and it was mad and crazy and exhilarating. One morning Patrice called and said, "Let's all go to Cancun." We did not have time to pack or to clean up, but we were there that evening. We bought things in Cancun and sat in the water where the Mayan people sat a thousand years before, and looked through water so clear that you could see 100 fathoms to the bottom.

We scuba dived, even Lila, who was like a fish in the great ocean and had fins for legs when she swam.

We stayed in a place of considerable beauty, a place that belonged to a friend and was so secluded that the local busy bodies stayed away. I began to have compassion that summer for the famous, and the terribly intrusive and public lives they were forced to live.

In the early morning, we went for a drive to the Mayan Temples by the ocean near Cancun and saw what an incredible civilization it had been. It had fallen because a few corrupt men had put their own needs and interests above those of everyone else.

Huge pyramids jutted out from the jungle, the moss and undergrowth constantly threatening to engulf them and to steal them away from civilization and return them to the jungle. Monkeys and other animals chattered as we walked to the top of the tallest pyramid and looked out across the Pacific in air so clean, we really thought that we could see China or some exotic place across the sea.

Patrice said to me one night, after Lila had fallen asleep and as we sat out on the balcony off the bedroom drinking something local which was sweet and powerful, "Sam, I want you to know that even though you cannot choose between Jennifer and me, that I have loved you more then I ever believed it possible to love anyone."

My heart skipped a beat and I turned to her and wanted to say something wonderful about how I felt about her, but she smiled a smile so brilliant that it blinded me and my mouth suddenly lost its bravery.

CHAPTER 17

The changes in Patrice over the next few weeks were very subtle. Had I known of the pressure she was under, I would have been much more sympathetic.

I discovered later that about this time, Manuel Gutierez had threatened to make Patrice leave the family house, a move so serious that it would have sent most women in Mexico into a psychiatric condition. It was the equivalent of being ostracized by the family.

Lila, however, noticed nothing different and began to like Patrice so much I was beginning to worry that her need for a mother was overtaking the loyalty she had for her own mother.

I would watch her with Patrice and my heart would break a little to think about what she had gone through in the past few years. A dying mother, a new father, the separation from her brother and her mother's friends and family and, now this, a substitute mother, one who was in many ways as wonderful, and as romantic, and special as the one she replaced.

Patrice joined my class when we went to Mexico City for a meeting with Don Carlos Obriggon, grandson of the former President of Mexico and the leading psychologist in the country. It was only through Jean 's magical intervention that we were able to meet with him.

He was quite old now, perhaps in his late eighties, and he no longer went to his office at the university but stayed at his home near the outdoor park where they sold paintings and jewelry on Saturdays, an area of Mexico City not unlike Greenwich Village in New York or Soho in London.

When he found out that Patrice was with our group, he kissed her hand and told my class in Spanish that we were in the presence of the greatest poet of Mexico, and probably one of two or three of the great poets of our time.

Patrice was gracious and shy in his presence. He was, after all, a very great man and, unlike America which made its heroes into buffoons and idiots, Mexico revered its heroes even if what they were now doing to Patrice was nasty and mean-spirited.

Don Carlos spoke of the impact of the Freudians on Latino psychotherapy and the relevance of dreams in a country that believed in the magic of the spirit. Freud, he told us, was the godfather of Mexican therapy. You could not begin to understand Mexico without first reading Freud.

My students, who did not believe in magic, were respectful but their need for logic and for ready answers to difficult questions made them hear without understanding.

When he was done with his presentation, Don Carlos served us wine in beautiful glasses and his wife passed around little canopies filled with sweet jams and honey. I thanked him for his presentation and he responded, amused, that my students were much like his students. They were in a rush to get answers without knowing how to ask the correct questions.

He touched Patrice's hand and said to her that she must be strong and weather the storm. It would pass, as it always did in Mexico. She would be stronger for the experience, even if it did not seem so in the moment.

Patrice kissed him on the cheek, took a book from her handbag and gave it to him. I discovered later that it was a book of the poems she had read to me this summer, the most intimate poems she had ever written and the reason for the attacks on her from the left. She had inscribed in the book, Don Carlos told me later, "To Don Carlos Obriggon, the soul of Mexico, our father and mentor."

Don Carlos read the inscription and was very moved. He took the book to his wife and showed it to her. His wife looked up at Patrice and smiled and nodded to her. In Mexico such a nod meant that one had entered the ranks of friendship and that you would be welcome in this home whenever you needed a place of rest or a sanctuary.

Later in the day we saw the Diego Rivera murals at the National Palace and saw how Rivera had changed his depiction of Cortez from victor and benefactor in the initial panel to syphilitic fool and tyrant in the last. The murals spanned thirty years and much had happened in Rivera's life in that time to change his thinking.

The National Palace, like much of the central part of Mexico City, was built on the site of a lake which had been filled by the Aztecs with boats of gravel and sunk to the bottom of the lake to form a land fill. The buildings sank into the soft gravel and all the buildings in this area were on the original site of the magnificent Aztec City, which was ultimately sacked by Cortez and were sinking, some as much as nine feet. The edge of the National Palace had a cracked foundation and was closed off for fear of breaking away and hurting someone.

Across from the National Palace was the National Cathedral. It too had sunk and scaffolding inside kept it from breaking apart. We looked at the Black Christ in one of the many chapels and heard Patrice tell the story of how the father of a daughter had put poison on the Black Christ and the lover of his daughter had kissed the statue after prayer and had died from the poison. When that happened, the statue turned black.

I looked at Patrice to see if the story had impacted her at all but I saw nothing to make me think so.

Across the street from the National Palace and the Cathedral was the Zocolo where today they held a demonstration against the government. Cardinas, the Socialist candidate in the 1988 election, which everyone thought had been stolen from him, led the demonstration. He was the son of the President who had permitted Trotsky into the country and I stood and listened to him speak for awhile. He had a wonderful voice and his message made my heart beat a little faster. End poverty, stop corruption, make Mexico great. Who could argue with any of that?

Before we ate dinner, we went to the Diego Rivera Museum and saw the home of the great muralist. He had been at war with the Communists when he used his prestige to get Trotsky admitted to Mexico after Stalin had a death contract placed out on his life. Trotsky paid back his kindness by having an affair with Frida Kahlo, Rivera's beautiful but tragic wife.

A painting by Frida Kahlo is particularly symbolic of this moment in my relationship with Patrice. It has her beautiful and serene face on the body of a deer. The deer is running through a forest and it has arrows stuck in it and is bleeding huge drops of blood.

You could not see the painting which I saw hanging in the Diego Rivera Museum that day and not feel for the women of the ages who carry such complex expectations inside of them that it is a wonder they survive the day to day battles we all must face in our lives.

It is how I felt for Patrice as we drove home from Mexico City that evening, the rain pounding our bus and the driver humming a song to keep from losing control on the wet and curving road to Cuernavaca.

Patrice snuggled up against my body, tired from our long day and kissed my head. "It was a good day, Sam, but Mexico City drains the spirit and I am so very tired."

We both were tired, but somehow in the way she spoke, for the first time since I'd known her, there was resignation in her voice.

I asked what Don Carlos had meant when he said that she must be brave.

"Ah, Sam, Mexico is such a little place. We know each others business. The critics are suddenly unkind to me. They love you and then they hate you. It is the way of Mexico. They will love me again, but not for awhile. I must get used to it."

I didn't understand then about the politics of it all or how easily the critics and the judges of competitions could be bought off in Mexico. The family was putting its pressure on Patrice to marry Juan Guzman and to stay as far away from the American professor as was humanly possible.

To me, family was the ballast and support you got in life that helped you overcome adversity. If you strayed or were not perfect, you were still within the fold. But in Mexico there was a fearsome price for straying. I was only now beginning to see how costly it could be for everyone involved.

The bus rolled on through the night and we sat in the dark and planned our next adventure. I was just happy to be with Patrice and we could have gone to the neighborhood store and it would have been thrilling.

CHAPTER 18

I spent a great deal of time with Lila and Partner the next few days. Although they enjoyed the summer and were so busy it probably did not matter, I felt that I had not been spending enough time with them.

And so we did up the town, as they would say, and saw more of Cuernavaca in a few days than we'd seen in a month. For *comida* one day, we went to the beautiful Maxamilian Gardens where the Austrian ruler of Mexico kept his mistress during the summer months when Cuernavaca housed the rich and powerful.

The gardens were in a lush and beautiful residential section of Cuernavaca, and wild birds ran up to greet us when we walked in and the waiters took our order with a pen made from the feather of an exotic bird.

The tradition of the importance of birds in Mexico is an ancient one. An early ruler of Mexico began the practice of measuring ones wealth by the number of feathers of an exotic and rare bird one had in his or her possession. The name of the bird alludes me for my mind was filled with other thoughts just then.

We sat in splendor and looked at the lush and manicured grounds. Lila and Partner walked around the gardens and looked at the stone sculptures Maxamilian had placed on the grounds during his brief term as emperor. Another European to plunder and steal, I thought, but then everyone took more from Mexico than they ever gave in return.

You could not come here and not take the beauty, and the culture, and the joy of life back with you. And if it made a difference in your life, than you were blessed by the gods and you would come back again and again until it was in your soul and you could not have stayed away even if you tried.

Lila ordered her meal in her improving Spanish and the waiter smiled and nodded at me.

"This is a pretty place, dad", Lila said, sipping on her drink. "Patrice would like to come here, I'll bet."

I nodded in agreement. "I'll bet she would," I said, and looked at the door inadvertently to see if she was there.

But I knew that she had left for a short stay in the south of Mexico, in Chiapas Province, were the native rebellion was still raging against the Mexican government. She was on a human rights panel and had been asked to join a fact-finding group to see if a solution to the problems could be found.

I was very proud of her and would have liked to have asked the critic who called her a "Rich Bitch" to join her if he had the guts. It was very dangerous in the south and I was worried for her when she told me about her trip.

"Do not worry for me, Sam," she said. "Cry for the children of Chiapas who go hungry and do not see the daylight because they are blinded early in life because of the malnutrition."

I looked over at my beautiful daughter and wondered if she would write poetry or join the cause for human rights. She was Jennifer's daughter and I knew that she would. But the arrogance of the very intelligent can fool you and who could ever know the road a child would decide to travel?

We sat in the Maxamilian Gardens and ate our very nice food and watched the wild birds run about squawking and making outlandish noises. It always amazed me that God could make animals so beautiful and yet give them such harsh and unpleasant voices. But maybe that was the way he intended it. Beauty was nothing without a similar voice. And how few of us could boast of such a thing?

Jennifer, for certain, whose voice was strong and clear and true before her illness, my daughters Rachel and Lila, and now, Patrice, who had a voice to send chills up and down your spine when she read her poetry.

> Cry for the children of Chiapas
> and all children who live in darkness.
> Stand strong and hold your ground,
> my beautiful Patrice,
> and do not let them take the light
> from your smile.

I missed her in that moment and I would have walked through the jungles to be with her. And then I realized that Lila was talking and that I had heard nothing she had said. I turned my thoughts of Patrice off and listened again to my daughter who was saying to me in that moment that it made her feel bad to eat so well when the poor children had so little.

Who says that there is not a connection between the souls of people?

On the drive back after *comida*, I could not help but notice that all of the homes in this area of town where the wealthy lived had huge walls and gates surrounding them. Was it to keep the intruders out, I wondered, or was it to keep the troubled and often distorted family lives of the people within from escaping?

I could only wonder at the pressures being placed on Patrice by her family. Did they stop talking to her as my parents had done when I had displeased them? I hoped not. It was the singularly most awful memory of my childhood to have my talkative and gregarious parents suddenly treat me as if I were a leper.

But who could ever know the secrets of a family, or the truly cruel things they could do to the very people they claimed to love?

Don Carlos Obriggon had said something else to Patrice when he told her to be brave, but I had not given it much credence until this moment. He said, "The great Indian poet Gomez, do you know him?"

Patrice shook her head.

"Well, it does not surprise me. They murdered him during the revolution for his opposition to the genocide they were practicing. In any event, Gomez wrote, 'Do not walk from you family, my child, for they are the lifeline to the heart. But do not take so seriously their desires that you forget who you are. Should you do that, then you will be as they are and you will have their fears and their hatreds."

I thought Don Carlos was encouraging Patrice to stand up against her parents, but as we drove by the walled in homes of the wealthy, I realized that Gomez was writing about the very rich and the strangle hold they had on Mexico. If Patrice went in her own direction, she would not be of the family and they would discard her as they did the dirty linen and yesterday's news. Without a moment of remorse.

A troubled system never permits opposition. It was a truth of therapy. I should have known it then, but the beauty of the day distorted my view and we sped on to our next adventure, my daughter radiant in the back seat with Partner, chattering away about her next great adventure with Patrice.

CHAPTER 19

It was to be our last trip together before my return home. School started in California and I could not have prolonged the stay even if I had wanted to, and I did.

Cuernavaca was more beautiful the last few weeks of our visit than it had ever been. It rained during the late afternoon and early evening, and then the air would cool and the nights were fresh and full of the electricity everyone felt who came to the City of Eternal Spring.

It was a tropical city, and if I knew more about plants and flowers, I would describe the lushness that surrounded us wherever we went. The Institute had a swimming pool, but we had been there a week before we realize where it was. The banana trees and tropical plants were so thick and lush that they all but hid it from view.

During breaks from our classes, Lila and Partner and I would walk a block past the Autobus Estrella, one of the many large and small bus stations in the city, across the intersections of Morelos and Benito Juarez, and to the bakery. There, we were engulfed by the smells of Mexican pastry.

You picked up a tray and put whatever you chose onto the tray with metal tongs. Lila always chose something very sweet and my pledge to Jennifer that she eat only healthy food would take a nose dive in those moments. But the truth was that you did not tempt a child with pastry and then deny it to them. So I allowed her to take apple filled sweet rolls and sometimes the sugary pretzel-like pastries which had a name that I could never remember. I called them Mexican *Challahs*, after the twisted Jewish bread we ate on the Sabbath, and the name stuck.

We would walk back to the Institute with our goodies from the bakery and have a glass of milk or a cup of thick coffee with sweet cream. I do not think in reality that I was ever as happy as I was in those moments with Lila, sitting with my students and the other instructors, gossiping or discussing more serious things, and eating our Mexican *Challahs* and drinking sweet coffee.

Sometimes when she was there, Patrice would join us. She taught a class on Latino poets which I was tempted to attend, but since our initial meeting, we had an unspoken agreement not to intrude on one another's class.

She would kiss me on the cheek, and look happily into my eyes, and whisper things in my ear. I would look at her each time we were together and her beauty would be like the discovery of a new continent or like landing on the moon, it had such an impact.

On certain days, the jewelers or the weavers would come to the Institute and lay their goods out by the snack bar where we sat, near the pool. Lila would always buy something inexpensive and even Patrice admitted that her taste was extraordinary for so young a child. Sometimes Patrice would help me buy gifts for my friends in California, showing me how to tell the good from the bad.

I would never bargain with the vendors and made a policy for the family that we would pay them whatever they asked. It was an undignified practice, I said, to hassle people who lived so close to the edge when we had so much more than they did. And I still feel that way and shudder when people tell me about the way they bargained the vendors down on their trips to Mexico. It made me think of the time someone in my neighborhood told my mother that they had "Jewed" someone down in a transaction and my mother, who hadn't a harsh word for anyone, said that they had to leave the house and that using such a word in her home was a violation of the home and the people in it.

Patrice kissed me on the cheek in front of everyone when I told her my policy, and the young Spanish teachers giggled and clucked, but in Patrice's presence they were respectful in a way that Mexican women are when someone very special is in their midst.

In class one day I spoke of the power of the Mexican family to control the lives of their children. One of the students, more familiar with Mexico than the others, showed me an article in a local paper about Patrice. It described her family difficulties and said that she had always been a headstrong woman, but that people with her talent sometimes were permitted special considerations which were not necessarily good for them in the long run. The article urged her to give up her North American paramour…it is the word they used…and return to her senses.

I was incensed. I would have punched the writer out in a second if I could.

I waited for Patrice to finish her poetry class and showed her the article. She shrugged. She was familiar with it and with others that had been published.

"We need to talk, Patrice," I said.

She looked at me in that amused way of hers, and nodded. "You are right, Sam. We do need to talk," and we agreed to meet later at the condo when Lila had gone to sleep.

Lila and Partner and I skipped *comida* at home that day and drove with Jean Henry to the Hacienda de Cortez, a very old estate which had gone through many changes since it originally made sugar from sugar beets in the early days of the Spanish conquests. Sugar to feed the insatiable appetite of the new world and to sweeten the rum and other liquors was worth almost as much as the gold the conquistadors searched so hard for, but could not find. The City of Lost Gold turned out to be a myth. The sugar to make liquor was very real as was the practice of slavery, which was used for a time on the sugar beet plantations.

The Hacienda de Cortez had a long, tree-lined driveway that led to the beautiful old estate which had, after many different lives, including its partial destruction in the revolution, been turned into a small hotel and restaurant.

We parked the van Jean drove and walked through the hotel to the beautiful old swimming pool, which had broken parts of a viaduct sticking out of the pool like ancient petrified trees. I learned for a sign near the pool that the viaducts had been built in 1539, only a few years after the conquest of Mexico by Cortez.

Lila put on her swim suit and imitated a fish while Jean and I took a drink at the pools edge and watched the children in the pool cavort about like little dolphins.

"So, boychick," she said, finally, "no romance this summer?"

"Come on, Jean," I said, "Let's not talk about it, huh? We're just friends."

"Easy for you to say, Sam. Manuel Gutierez is not your partner, and the whims of family life in Mexico are far from your concern. But they touch me, and I have to tell you the truth, Sam. When you leave for California, forget Patrice. It would be best for everyone."

I drank my drink slowly and looked over at her, but she looked straight ahead at the children in the pool. I wanted to tell her to mind her own business, but it was her business and I could not be mean to someone I had known and liked for so long, so I said nothing in response.

We like to think that words have such power that they can be used like swords. But sometimes it's better to be still and let the thoughts form before lashing out in anger. And so I said nothing, nor did Jean. She had said her piece, I guess, and a woman like Jean did not like to repeat herself.

I watched Lila swim for awhile until I finally jumped in the water with her and we played the game she loved called speed boat, where I would grab hold of her and push her through the water as fast as I could, making the sounds of a speed boat, while Partner ran along the side of the pool barking up a storm.

Later, we had an extraordinary meal at the restaurant that had once been the stables in the time of Cortez, and now was partially open to the outside. We had the salty beef, which is a specialty in the state of Morelos, and wine, and wonderful bread and cheese. It was a glorious meal, and the always welcome mariachi's came over and sang a song called, "Por Un Amor." It went:

Por un Amor
(For a love)
I cannot sleep and I live full of passion.
I have a love
that left forever in my life a bitter pain.
I have cried little drops of blood
from my wounded heart.
You have left my soul stricken
without compassion.
How much suffering can I bear?

The last line went in Spanish, "*He llorado gottitas de sangre del corrado. Me has dejado con el alma herida sin compasion.*"

Jean looked over at me and shook her head. How life imitated art, or was it the other way around?

Jean drove us home after lunch and dropped us off at the huge *Mercado*. Lila wanted to buy gifts for her teachers and for her classmates. Nowhere in Cuernavaca were there more items to buy then in the *Mercado* where the crowds jostled you and you could buy *molé* (a sauce made partially of chocolate) in large chunks which hung from the ceiling of the small shops.

We walked through the large building with exotic smells and the sounds of the people. An evangelist was praying over a loud speaker and kept calling on the name of The Senior, *Jesoos Kristay* to lead the people to the gates of heaven. It was only when I thought of it that I realized he was speaking of Jesus Christ, and we stopped and listened for awhile. Lila was enthralled and did not want to leave. Finally, however, we left when people started to speak in tongues and she became frightened.

We walked the huge building buying the small gifts she needed to give because we were leaving soon, when it hit me that my relationship with Patrice would become a long distance relationship just as it had been with Jennifer. It was surely the definition of hell, and I did not think, in all honesty, that I could manage another one.

Someone yelled out in Spanish, *Zapatas!* (shoes). It seemed like one of those words so appropriate to the moment. I was walking out, in a way. I was walking back to California and a life very different from the one I had with Patrice. I didn't want to think about it, but I did, and the rest of the day was spent in a haze.

We took a cab home, I might add. No one who shops at the *Mercado* has the energy to wait for a bus. No one, that is, but the poor people who have no alternative, and who spend their day at the beck and call of other people.

Zapatas, I kept thinking on the cab ride home, shoes.

CHAPTER 20

Jean came over and sat with Lila while I went to Las Mañanitas to meet Patrice. She looked utterly worn out from yet another day of fighting with everyone who came to Mexico on a shoe string, but wanted the Institute to house them with the families who had maids to serve them *comida*.

I felt badly for her, and we sat on the deck and had a margarita while I let her blow off the accumulated steam from the day. I don't think she would have been so happy to stay with Lila had she known where I was going that evening. When she asked, I mumbled something about a student meeting. She was too tired to ask anymore.

Patrice and I sat outside on a table in a secluded spot and listened to the birds shriek and hiss at one another. They seemed to be in a particularly bad mood tonight. Why should they be any different than anybody else, I thought?

I didn't know where to start, so we sat for awhile in that uncomfortable place where we each wanted to talk but no one had the courage to say anything.

Finally, I said, very tentatively, at first, "Patrice, I think I'm starting to understand what you're going through because of our relationship. Don't you think that we should talk about it? It does have to do with me and I feel responsible for what you're going through."

Patrice looked away and sat for awhile in thought.

"I do not know what to tell you, Sam," she said, finally. "I have been dreading this moment since I was a teenager. They have made no big point of it before, and most of me did not think that they were serious, but with the economy being what it is in Mexico, the families are very worried. They see my marriage as a way to consolidate their power base, I suppose."

"And where will that leave you, Patrice?" I asked, looking at her as directly as you could look at woman of such overpowering beauty.

"I will not stop seeing you, Sam. Do you not know that? I thought that it was so very evident that I didn't think it needed to be said."

It was the tone in her voice that made me stop and not say anything for awhile. She was hurt.

"In America," I said, "we always try and clarify what may be unclear. It is our way, baby, and I am really no different, really. I need clarity."

"Aw, Sam," she said, taking my hand and putting it to her face. "What can I say to make you understand how I feel about you? I know that I love you with everything I possess. I know that I will see you no matter what. I know that I will never consummate a marriage with anyone but you, never. We are as one, Sam. You will come to see that when you are gone, and you will be able to put thoughts of Jennifer aside, and then we can love one another. There is no more that anyone can say."

Ah, so easy, but it wasn't and I told her that I couldn't manage loving two women. Jennifer was as alive in my heart as ever, and Patrice needed to move on in her life and do what she needed to do without thoughts of us being together. I had a child whose mother had recently died. How could I be with someone else without alienating my child and the memory of her mother?

And then I told her was about the dark period I'd had when Jennifer would no longer see me. I told her about the long period of time when I was in hell, and what it was like in that dark and evil place. I told her that I could not stop myself from loving Jennifer during that time and how, in the 4 years when Jennifer would not see me, that each night before I went to bed, I could not be absolutely certain that I wanted to live through the night.

Patrice nodded her head slightly as I spoke about Jennifer. She looked at me and I could feel a shiver go through my body and then, without so much as a break in our conversation, she told me about the pressures of her family. Their behavior had alienated her so much from them that she was thinking of moving to California with me. She could not write in Mexico with such conduct from her family. She told me that Manuel, her brother, was behind the awful things that were being done to her, and that she had cursed him one night and they had almost come to blows. She said that she could not live in Mexico any longer and that the papers and the gossip would destroy her if she did.

But, she told me, as we held hands at our secluded table, not to think for a moment that it would not be worse if she gave in and married Juan Guzman. It would be the hell of a lifetime, like the hell I'd suffered, but worse, because it would continue on until she died. She would have none of it, she said. If she had learned anything in America, it was about freedom. And she said it in Spanish, enunciating each syllable. *Li-ber-dad! Liberdad!* Freedom. It was a beautiful word, however it was said.

The wind blew one of the shudders against the side of the hotel wall as she said the words.. It sounded like a cannon shot. *Liberdad*!!…Freedom!!…My life!!…

She told me the nasty things that several families had done to her friends to get them to marry their chosen men. She was ready for it, she said. She had listened for many years now, and she knew the way Mexican families got their ounce of flesh. It would not happen to her.

She told me about Chiapas, which we had not really discussed, and cried at the brutality of the Mexican soldiers. She knew the commanding officer and could not believe that he was capable of such butchery. They had played together as children and he was a loving and compassionate father. How could he do such terrible things?

"They kill children, Sam. I am embarrassed for my country. We have forgotten the spirit of the revolution. We are ruled by tyrants. It will destroy us, I fear."

Could she live in America, I asked?

"I do not know," she said. "A writer must be where the people and events are he writes of. I do not know if I can leave forever, Sam. It is truthfully how I feel. But for awhile I could leave. We must discuss it more.

Mexico, I thought as I drove home to my child. It was such a place of beauty, but the cruelty ran deep and the pain that could be done to those you loved was awful to behold.

I went to Lila's room and watched my daughter sleep. She had a happy look on her face. Above her bed she had placed pictures she had drawn of all of the places we had visited.

Next to me she had a huge heart with an arrow through it to signify, I guess, love. And she had one next to Patrice, as well, whose name she had written under the picture, but she had spelled it, Patrees.

It was a picture of us in the ocean. Dolphins leaped from the ocean and Lila drew happy faces on each and every one.

I made myself a margarita and sat in the living room and thought about the extraordinary night I had just had, starring out of the window into the night, wondering about the extraordinary things that were happening to me. I thought about Patrice and knew, in my heart, that we were at an impasse, one which could never have a good resolution.

In time, I went to sleep and dreamt wonderful dreams of flying fish with happy faces on them and Patrice next to me speaking to them in Spanish as if it was the most natural of things to do.

Partner came over to me before I went to sleep.

"Hello boy," I said, "I love you, my special, my wonderful dog.

But he just laid back and stretched himself out on the floor. He was used to the emotionality of old men, and just laid there and took it in his stride.

CHAPTER 21

We went to Cozumel for our final adventure. We did not see smiling dolphins with happy faces, but we went deep sea fishing and I felt like a Hemingway character whose inner soul and spirit were being tested by the way they handled themselves with the big fish.

Patrice sat on the boat in a bikini with a huge hat to shield her face from the brilliant sun, watching me struggle with the great fish on the other end my line. She confided in me later that she had learned many new words in English that they had not taught her at Radcliff or Sara Lawrence by watching me do battle with the great fish on my line.

"My brave North Dakota fisherman," she kept saying when I would say another of those new words, and then I would return to the joy of fighting a fish I did not hate and who had done nothing at all to me.

Finally, I got the fish in and the crew came around to see the monster fish of the deep that had taken me an hour to catch. It was a 20 pound Grouper, probably the most lethargic fish in the ocean. Patrice brought me over a drink and chatted with me to cover the laughter from the crew.

We sailed the seas that weekend living on a large sailboat with lovely quarters. The crew took to Lila and, if ever there was a natural born sailor, it was she. She loved the bounce of the ocean and the power of the wind against the sail. Partner was another story and, unfortunately, got a tad sea sick. The poor dog would not even come out to eat the scraps of the meat we would leave, or to play with Lila.

I found a love poem in the Songs of Solomon one evening and read it to Patrice as we sat in lounging chairs on the ship's deck, the sea running smoothly beneath our sailing ship. It went:

Awake, O North Wind,
and come, O South wind!
Blow upon the ocean
that its fragrance may be
wafted aboard.
Let my beloved come to this
ship
and touch my face.

I had taken liberties with Solomon's beautiful lines, but I did not think that he would mind. And Patrice replied to me:

I am the rose of Sharon,
a lily of the valleys.
O, my dove, in the clefts of the rock
in the covert of the cliff,
let me see your face,
let me hear your voice:
for your voice is sweet,
and your face is lovely.

One day we docked in a small fishing village and went to an art gallery owned by a friend of Patrice's who served us lunch on the balcony of her studio overlooking the ocean. She showed Patrice an article that had come out in a magazine very supportive of Patrice and her struggle. The article said:

"Patrice Gutierez fights the struggle of all men and women of Mexico who will not yield to the whims of their family. In this struggle, we must unite and support her, for the victory means that Mexico will be a modern and just nation, and that the barbaric practice of arranged marriages will end."

Patrice became teary eyed for a moment and thanked her friend for her kindness. Her friend, I was to discover, lived here in exile for precisely the reason Patrice was being made to feel so guilty for her act of defiance.

Her friend, Salina, told us a sad story of being made to leave the family home in Mexico City and of her old grandmother wailing in the night as she snuck off alone. She had not seen or heard from her family in five long and lonely years.

We sat for a long while saying nothing, looking at the floor.

When we returned to the boat, we immediately left port and headed for a calm bay to scuba dive. I was happy to leave the fishing village, although it was a lovely old Mayan city and it deserved more than a brief, but sad visit.

We spent the rest of our time on the boat scuba diving, swimming, and eating the wonderful food prepared by the crew, all of whom seemed to be magicians when it came to preparing our meals. Sometimes they would cook the fish that Lila caught over a grill, and it was always delicious.

At the end of the day, we would sit on the deck of the boat and watch the sun set over the Pacific. It was like a huge fireball. As it sank into the ocean, its effect on us all was magical. We could not talk. We had witnessed something so beautiful that words would have ruined it.

At night, Patrice and I listened to the crew sing love songs. One of the men played beautiful old Mexican songs on the guitar and his voice was full of the sad and plaintive sounds of someone who knew the suffering that love could bring when it did not go well.

The boat rocked to its own rhythms in the ocean and we rose and fell with it as naturally as the sun, and the moon, and the wind are as one with the sea.

Mi corazon, mi corazon, the sailor sang, *es quebrado.* My heart, my heart is broken. *En sus brazos es mi futuro.* In your arms is my future.

That weekend was idyllic. We would sit on deck and drink coffee in the morning, the ocean breeze cool enough to wear a jacket. Our faces were tanned and rosy from the sun.

As I sit thinking of that weekend, I think of a song Solomon wrote so many thousands of years ago.

> I slept, but my heart was awake.
> I sought her, but found her not.
> I called her, but she gave no answer.
> If you find my beloved, tell her this:
> I am faint with love.

Chapter 22

It did not happen all at once or in any way that I can tell you had a beginning. It was gradual and slow and it had a mind of its own.

I felt it before we left Mexico. They had a going away party for us, but Patrice could not come. She had a reason and it sounded fine, and I would have believed her, if I could. Calls went unanswered, and when she would finally call back, it would seem fine, but it wasn't.

Something in her eyes began to show the tensions she was under and she often had a far away look on her face.

I did not know at the time of the transformation going on inside of her or of the growing imbalances she was experiencing. I knew that she was somehow different, but then the strong and wonderful parts of her would show themselves and I would not see what my training and my experiences should have helped me to see.

I did not know that such a very great poet as Patrice, someone who lived within the sensibilities of their inner world and experienced life in a way so very different from you and me, I did not know that they broke in ways much like the way we broke. I thought that they were super human and could take anything, but I was wrong.

About this time, Patrice was asked to leave the house of her family. I was no longer an issue. I was returning to America and I did not matter to Manuel Gutierez, or to the Guzman family, or to the gossip mongers or the envious critics who had less talent in their whole bodies then she had in her left little finger.

What mattered was that Patrice had said publicly that she would not marry Juan Guzman and that she did not love him. She also said that the practice of arranged marriages was barbaric and it should be prohibited.

For this, she was placed in exile, and it broke her spirit.

She came to stay with us in California shortly after we returned to the states, but she was miserable and could not write. She would stare at the wall and sit for hours without moving.

In my sorrow I asked an Hispanic colleague of mine, Mina Garza, to see Patrice in the hope that someone with a common heritage and language might be able to help. But it was not to be and Mina told me that Patrice was moving into a very deep depression and possibly needed hospitalization.

I could not believe that just weeks earlier we had sat on the bow of a sailing ship holding one another and reciting poetry, but Mina correctly pointed out that Patrice had been fighting an unwinable battle with, not only her family, but with her culture. She may have seemed well outwardly, but inwardly, she was in great turmoil throughout the entire time we had been together. When the turmoil become too great, Mina noted, Patrice had begun slipping gradually into a great void. If she stayed in it, she might never come out of it. The voyage was an inner voyage and no one could know without seeing inside of her soul whether the voyage was complete.

I tried to talk to her, we all did, but she sat in a chair and stared at nothing. Gradually, she seemed to be losing awareness of who she was. Finally, I called Harriet Gutierez because I could not speak to Manuel and said that Patrice needed to be hospitalized. I asked her to speak to Mina Garza who, I explained, was an excellent psychotherapist and who had worked closely with Patrice and knew her condition as well as anyone. Some hours later, plans were made for Patrice to return home. Mina would accompany her on the flight.

We were all very sad when she left. Lila cried in her room and would not come out for dinner.

At the airport, I held Patrice, but something went limp in her body and I knew the great strength of character, the power I had always felt inside of her, was no longer there.

I watched her walk to the plane, Mina holding her arm to guide her, her eyes very far away as if she were viewing some scene which was hidden from the rest of us.

When she left, I went to bed and my little girl came in to comfort me.

"Will we ever see Patrice again?" Lila asked.

I could only shake my head and say, "I don't know, baby, I just don't know."

Partner sat in a corner and wailed for a long while. He had come to love Patrice, just as we had.

One day at work I received a call from Manuel Gutierez. I was cold and aloof on the phone as one might expect. He said that Patrice had been sent to a hospital in Texas. She was very depressed, he said, and they were considering electric shock treatment, which sometimes helped reduce depression but could affect memory.

Manuel began crying on the phone and said he knew he had made a mistake and had told Patrice that it didn't matter what she did as far as the marriage. But it was too late, and she had fallen into a deep depression and could not be brought out it.

I said some not very nice things to Manuel and called him names that probably were not fair given his grief. But finally I agreed to see Patrice at the hospital in Texas and to help as much as I could.

I will tell you that my own mental health was not good at this time. I was heart sick at what had happened to Patrice. It seemed unnecessary and so mean-spirited of God to do this to me twice. I did not honor God in those weeks and months, but said some terrible things to him because of my grief.

But I flew down and saw Patrice one hot Texas day in October, four months from the day when I had first met her in Jean Henry's office.

The nurse brought her to me and I was shocked when I saw her. I am far from certain that she recognized me or if she knew that anyone was even present. Her eyes were empty, like small lifeless holes, and she rocked herself to some song that only she could hear. I touched her hand, but it was cold and unresponsive. She was, for all that one could say about life, no longer alive, but in a world of despair where the mind is placed in suspension and the outside world does not exist.

I stayed for two days. The staff was gracious, and kind, and treated me well. The Gutierez family had called to tell the staff that I was coming and that I had their support in this visit.

We discussed the many treatment options available, but what it amounted to was that Patrice was on some inner journey. When she had finished and was safely across the great sea that divided her mind, then and only then would she be back among the living. It was possible, said one doctor, that she would never make it home, but would stay forever in a state of suspended reality. His words.

I suppose in this day of political correctness that suspended reality was preferable to insanity, and that the rich and famous patients at the hospital and their families preferred the words. But to me, Patrice was no longer sane and words like suspended reality sounded hollow and hopeless.

I remember sitting in the hospital on the second day of my visit and someone gave me a bible. I leafed through it and found in the writing of King David the following description of what I guessed Patrice was experiencing.

> You have put me in the depths of the Pit,
> in the region dark and deep.
> I am like those who have no hope,
> like those whom you remember no more,
> like the slain that lie in the grave.

At the end of my stay in Texas, I saw Patrice again but she was in a world of her own, which was inaccessible to me. I sat with her for most of the day and read her the beautiful poetry she had written, but not an eye twittered or a cell in her face showed any sign of change and, at the end of the day, I flew back to California, heart sick and morose.

I called Manuel Gutierez when I returned and told him that only the most extraordinary act of will would bring Patrice back to us. She was so far into a world of her own that no one could know when, or if, she would free herself.

I told Manuel to go to Patrice and stay with her, and to hold her, and to speak to her of the love he had inside, the love he brought from Mexico, and the love of her friends and family, and the love of everyone who had read her poetry and had been touched by it. I was not inclined to believe that he would do it, for he was a very rigid and unloving man.

But he did. He flew to Texas and brought pictures of her youth and the greetings of her family, friends, and her adoring readers, who were vast and remained endlessly hopeful for her. He brought the worried articles the formerly hostile critics had written asking God to help her recover. He brought the poems and the writings from when Patrice was a young girl and read them to her.

And he did something else, something extraordinary for an educated man. He brought a *Curandero* to Texas with him, a faith healer, and between them, they help Patrice walk across the void and to see the land where trees blew in the wind, and the sky rose forever, and the horizon was filled with hope.

And slowly, Patrice moved out of her illness and back to recovery, although everyone knew that she would never be her old self but someone new who had evolved during her secret trip across the geography, the mountains and the valleys of the soul.

In late January, she was released from the hospital and returned to her family home in Cuernavaca, a celebrity. I saw pictures of her on the Spanish television network. She had changed, of course, and seemed more quiet and less certain. The flame that burned inside of her had dimmed, it seemed to me.

We were happy for her in my home and wrote her letters and called her as often as we could. Lila made her drawings at school. One drawings had Patrice waving goodbye to the doctor with a simple sentence underneath in Spanish which said," I can go home now, doctor. I am not sick anymore."

We spoke on the phone and her voice, though strained and tired, had a sweetness to it that lifted my heart. "I miss you, Sam," she said. "I knew you were in the hospital when you came to see me and I said *hola, mi amor* (Hello, my love) and told that you I loved you, but you did not hear me."

I felt a joy come over me that I'd not felt in months.

We made plans to meet in Mexico City, but when the time came, she was still too weak and the doctor called and said that she was very fragile and that we should not rush things too much.

She was at work on a project, she confided in me later, and when it was finished, she felt that it would be a very substantial work.

And, so it was. So great that when it came out, it caused an uproar in the Spanish and then the world wide press.

A review in the *New York Times Review of Books* said," The Mexican poet, Patrice Gutierez, has moved from the ranks of the very good to the ranks of the very great. Her book of poems, *Sentimiento*, about her love for an American she met one summer in Mexico, is a book for the ages. It is so beautiful that even the always troubling problem with translation cannot hide the fact that this is a book of a great writer and possibly the most beautiful love poetry ever written."

Patrice sent me the book before the press received it and only days before the early reviews came out. The dedication was to me and it said:

"To Sam, my beloved friend. You saved my life when I was troubled. You came to me in the midst of my darkness and you lifted me into the light. You are my love, my life, my *Beshert*, my destiny."

I called her to tell her how touched and moved I was by her poetry and what, I knew, she already understood: that the book was very great and that it would live on in time.

"I wrote it in the hospital," she said. "I began to write the poems when you came to see me. I wrote them in my head and, when I was well enough, I sat at a table in my mother's old room with the Cuernavaca sun coming in and the birds singing, and I wrote them down. I did not compose or have an uncertain word. I wrote them down as they were dictated to me by my mind."

The Spanish television network asked if they could interview me about the book Patrice had just written. I allowed them to come to my office at the university and to speak to me as long as we spoke only about the book. Our relationship was not to be discussed.

I told them in Spanish that the book Patrice had written was a book from the heart of a great artist. Anyone who knew Patrice knew of her warm heart and the beauty of her spirit.

"Patrice Gutierez," I said "has written of love with the insights that we are blessed with once or twice in a lifetime. She is of Mexico and of all Latinos, and I urge everyone who wishes to know of love and its greater meaning in life, to read her book and marvel at the glory of her creation."

I was asked about the dedication and whether I was not the man about whom the poems were written? I shook my head and said, "Patrice Gutierez writes of love, glorious, uplifting, incredible love. Not of me, but of all men and women who dare enter the realm of magic and who allow their souls to fly and soar on the wings of its' magical bird."

The interview was shown in Mexico, where it caused a stir and where I was said to have become a minor hero in a country that worships love but has such difficulty in showing it. At least that is what Patrice said to me in a voice which grew in strength each day.

Chapter 23

Lila and I went to see her that summer in her home in Cuernavaca. We flew down and she met us in Mexico City.

She looked wonderful, like her old self, and she had the magic back in her eyes and in her face, which had been gone for so long that I thought God had extinguished the flame in her heart.

In the airport, which is always crowded with an ocean of people, strangers came up to Patrice and touched her. Some of them said, "Thank God that you are well. Our prayers were answered." It happened time and again and Patrice was always warm and responsive, thanking each person in turn as if she had known them forever. In a way, perhaps she had, because a poet as great as Patrice surely seeks to know the hearts and souls of everyone of us.

We drove to Cuernavaca, across the mountain range and the pine trees, which were green and lush and, which fooled everyone who thought of Mexico as a place of cactus or palm trees. We stayed as guests of the Gutierez family. I could not put my animosity toward Manuel Gutierez aside, but it would have hurt Patrice if we had not stayed with her family. Manuel had tried to undue the harm he had done his sister. I had to give him that, but it was difficult for me to forgive him.

They were gracious and we had a wonderful time, but underneath it all, Patrice had changed. The small things that go on between a man and a woman, the looks, the touches, the jolts of electricity, they were no longer present.

I tried at first to tell myself that it was because of her illness and the voyage that she had been on. I tried to understand the way one is at the other end of hell. I had been there too, and I knew that had Jennifer walked back into my life then, if she had called and said, "Sam, I made a terrible mistake and I need you. Please come back into my life," I would have been there on the first plane I could find. And if that hadn't been soon enough, I would have walked to see her, to be with her, to touch her, to hold her, and to and feel her body against mine in the dark.

It was then that I knew her family had won her over.

You have great loves in your life, and family can be one of them. They tug at you and steal a kiss, or a hug, or a small concession all through your life. But in the end, you leave them and what they represent, and you gain your independence as a person, or it strangles you to death.

Patrice had come through the struggle, the rebellion, and the family had laid its claim on her soul even stronger than it had before she became ill. They made her ill and then they had brought her back and now, she was more firmly in the family than she had ever been. I could see that in the small ways she deferred to Manuel and how she was attentive to him in ways that she had not been before her illness.

On the second or the third day of our visit, we sat in her mother's room in Cuernavaca where she had written the wonderful love poems about our summer together. I remember the sun coming in and lighting the room, and how it sparkled and felt electric.

She began crying, and we sat together in her mother's room and watched the sun dance shadows across the walls. After awhile, when she had regained her composure, it was then that she told me of the epiphany, the deeply religious experience she'd had in the hospital in Texas.

"Sam, I saw Jesus. I did. And he told me to love my family. He said that I could love a man as well, but not as much as I love my family. He held out his hand to me, and when he touched me, I was better. He said he would not let go until I was well. He said that his Father had put me on earth to write the great poems that would touch the hearts and souls of men and women. Without my family, he said, I would be lost, like a lost soul wandering in the forest. He warned me that my talent would waste away, in time, and that I would not write the great things I was meant to write if I abandoned my family.

"I saw him, Sam. He had a beautiful face, so warm and kind that I could not stop looking at him, and he hurt, as I hurt, and he cried for me and prayed at night when I was lost and my soul was separated from my body. I promised him that I would love my family and put our differences behind us, and he made me well, Sam.

"It happened, Sam, it really did. And I met Jennifer, Sam, I met her one night. She waits for you, Sam, she waits in heaven for you and loves you with all of her might. I can never take her place, Sam. It would not be possible. I looked into her heart and it was so full of love for you that I would not think for a second that I could ever take her place."

And then she described Jennifer, and I knew that she had seen my love, and I began to cry with her. Perhaps from hurt, or perhaps it was from the joy of knowing that my Jennifer was well and that she waited for me, and that our love was timeless and that we would truly be as one in heaven.

She held me, and the sun touched our faces through the window of her mother's room.

For a few days, we tried to recapture our old life. We went to La India Bonita where the waitresses treated us like returning royalty, and to Las Mañanitas. We listened to the vendors hawk their wares, and to the to the chewing gum seller yelling, *"Chick-layyys, senor, chick-layyys."* But it wasn't the same and the magic had been replaced somehow by the ordinary. When Mexico begins to lose its magic, you have lost the soul of the place and you must leave before it is lost forever and will not return.

Patrice and I spent time together and Lila stayed with the friends she had met last summer at Las Hispañas. We had long talks about her work, held hands in the market, and shopped for presents. We had made the transition to a friendship and now felt at ease with one another.

We sat one evening at Las Mañanitas with the wild birds strangely quiet and a hush over the entire restaurant. It felt almost other-worldly to be there with Patrice that night.

She was more beautiful than ever and a maturity had come over her, a maturity bred of her struggle and defined by her newly found confidence.

"Sam," she said, looking at me in the light from the gas lamps that made everything full of shadows and out of focus, "there is something I did not tell you when we spoke."

I looked at her, held on to her hand, and waited for her to speak.

"I made a promise when I was ill, Sam. I made a promise to Jennifer that we would be friends, you and I, and that we would care for one another. I made a promise to her Sam, and it felt like a holy vow. I will not break my word to her.

"And she told me, Sam, that you are a man whose feelings were easily hurt, and that you would be angry if our feelings for one another changed, but that you were the most forgiving man she knew and that you would be a good and true friend to me all of my life."

I felt numb. I could not speak.

Where are the sweet flowers now, my love?
And the roses of our memories?
Don't cry for me, I am well
and in the safety of my heart
where spring is always and eternal,
like this place of beauty,
our paradise, our City of Eternal Spring.

CHAPTER 24

And that's what we became, in time, special friends. We wrote and we spoke on the phone. When she was in California, she came to see me or I would visit her in Mexico, and it was as natural between us as it was during our summer in Cuernavaca.

One night after we returned from Mexico, I told Lila that Patrice had seen her mother in a dream and of the conversation they'd had together, but she would not look at me and continued reading her book and playing with Partner.

One evening at dinner she told me that she knew her mommy had spoken to Patrice because her mommy told Lila in a dream to respect Patrice, for she was a wonderful woman and that her daddy had been blessed to have had her in his life.

But Lila was nothing if not stubborn and she would not warm up to Patrice when we were home because, I think, she blamed her for making Lila forget her mother and to think that someone could replace her. It was an act of disloyalty that Lila was still too young to forgive herself for, and she carried it around inside and felt the unforgiving guilt of a child whenever we were with Patrice.

Patrice went on to write other books of poetry, though none as beautiful or as powerful as *Sentimientos*. She had become a writer for the world and traveled constantly until she called, one day, to tell me that she would marry a childhood friend from Mexico and would I come for the wedding.

I declined, and I think she had not expected me to attend, but asked me out of a need for us to be honest with one another. Later, I found out that she'd had a child, a boy, and that she had named him Sam, but I discovered this only after I received a book of the poetry she had written after his birth. In the dedication it read:

"To my son Sam, who confirms my belief that love is passed on from the mother and the father to the child, and then, to the world."

She sent me a picture of her son, who looks like her, and who will become a handsome man, I am certain, given the very great beauty of his mother.

Lila and I talk about Patrice from time to time, but children have short memories and there are other things to occupy their thoughts.

I think of Patrice in a special place within my heart. I have been blessed with the love of two very great women. Few men can say that in a lifetime.

We still go to see Lila's mother and to say the prayers we have written for her. Lila is a beauty and has a mind that moves beyond her old fathers', and now writes her own prayers. The last one she wrote went:

"We are here, mommy, to honor your memory. We bring flowers to brighten your day and to add fragrance to your life. We love you everyday and miss you. Daddy cries sometimes at night because he misses you so much, and I cry too. We wish you were with us, but we know that we will see you in heaven. So don't be lonely. It won't be long. Daddy says that 50 years is like a second in heaven. We will see you in less then a second and we will have such fun together because we have a lot to tell you about, especially the summer in Mexico, and Patrice, and the poems she wrote about daddy.

"You said that daddy needed to meet someone, and he did. Someone special, but there isn't anyone as special as you, he says, and he misses you a lot, and he sometimes gets depressed at night and cries. But I come in and hold him, and he's a lot better.

"Anyway, Partner says hello, and my teacher said to tell you that I'm doing great in school. We have a happy house and lots of people come to visit, except for Patrice who doesn't remember us anymore, I think. Daddy says she's very busy, but I think I was right. She wasn't right for daddy, not like you were. She wasn't right and maybe she broke daddy's heart."

Maybe she did or maybe God meant for her to keep me company at a time when I was in grief over Jennifer. I don't know. I don't think love will come my way again, but like all of us, a small part of me hopes for the best and never closes the door to the improbable or to the unexpected.

My beard is grey now and I have aged, but my heart is firm and it is always possible that a true love to take me to old age will come into my life. More and more I think that Lila will be my great joy and companion in old age, but I should not burden her so.

I look at her every so often and pledge, on my soul, that she will never be so confined by the expectations of my needs to keep her from soaring as high as she can fly, for women must have *liberdad*, freedom, to go as high and as far as their vision of life will take them.

For the wonderful women in my life, for the truly wonderful women in the world who have the ability to fly, my heart is with you and I wish you God's speed. You have brightened my life and the life of every man worth his salt, and we should honor you every second, every minute, every hour, and every day of every year for your tender mercies.

How beautiful are you, my love,
how very beautiful.
There is no flaw in you.
Let me kiss you with the kisses
of my mouth.
I am my beloved's and my
beloved is mine;
she pastures her flock among
the lilies.

Set me as a seal upon your heart
as a seal upon your arm;
for love is as strong as death,
and passion as fierce as the grave.
Many waters cannot quench love
nor can floods drown it.

If we are offered love and turn it away,
we will be scorned.
For it flashes as a fire,
a raging flame.

-The End-

About the Author

Dr. Morley D. Glicken is the former Dean of the Worden School of Social Service in San Antonio; the founding director of the Master of Social Work Department at California State University, San Bernardino; the past Director of the Master of Social Work Program at the University of Alabama; and the former Executive Director of Jewish Family Service of Greater Tucson. He has also held faculty positions in social work at the University of Kansas and Arizona State University. Dr. Glicken received his BA degree in social work with a minor in psychology from the University of North Dakota and holds an MSW degree from the University of Washington and the MPA and DSW degrees from the University of Utah. He is a member of Phi Kappa Phi Honorary Fraternity.

Dr. Glicken has published six professional books on mental health issues for Allyn and Bacon/Longman Publishers, Sage Publications, and Lawrence Erlbuam and Associates. He published Ending the Sex Wars: A Woman's Guide to Understanding Men through iuniverse.

Dr. Glicken has published over 50 articles in professional journals and has written extensively on personnel issues for Dow Jones, publisher of the Wall Street Journal. He has held clinical social work licenses in Alabama and Kansas, and is a member of the Academy of Certified Social Workers. He is currently Professor Emeritus in Social Work at California State University, San Bernardino, and Executive Director of the Institute for Positive Growth: A Research, Treatment, and Training Institute in Los Angeles, California. The Institute's website can be found at: http://www.morleyglicken.com and Dr. Glicken can be reached online directly at mglicken@msn.com

To Spend Time in The City of Eternal Spring

For those of you who fell in love with Mexico after reading The City of Eternal Spring, Dr. Glicken leads workshop in Cuernavaca, Mexico. The workshops provide an opportunity to learn about and see Mexico, to develop beginning skill in Spanish, and to work on your creative writing.

Many people who have joined Dr. Glicken in Cuernavaca make life-long friends from among the several hundred people attending various programs each week. There are many opportunities to meet interesting people from the United States, Mexico, and from many other countries. Cuernavaca is an ideal place to visit since it has abundant restaurants, shops, galleries, and cultural events. Its close proximity to Mexico City allows for low cost travel, not only to Mexico City, but also to Acapulco, the silver city of Taxco, the enchanted city of Tepotzlan, and many other famous and exciting resorts, communities, and anthropological sites. Low cost field trips can be arranged to such places as the Anthropological Museum in Mexico City, the Pyramids of the Sun and the Moon, the homes of Diego Rivera and Frida Kahlo, and the famous murals by Diego Rivera at the Presidential Palace in Mexico City, to name just a few.

Dr. Glicken will help you find exciting places to eat, dance, and listen to wonderful music. You will never feel lonely or bored when you attend a Cuernavaca workshop and, like Sam, Jennifer, and Patrice, you never know when romance might enter your life. For more information about the workshops, please go to http://www.morleyglicken.com or contact Dr. Glicken directly at mglicken@msn.com

978-0-595-36373-5
0-595-36373-3